# WINGER

## GSU BOOK THREE

# LAURA JOHN

Cover Designer: Brittany Franks with Chaotic Creatives

Editor: BreathlessLit

Sensitivity Readers: J.P Jackson and Jennifer Demeter

# DEAR READER,

THIS BOOK HAS a few subjects that may not be easy for everyone to read so if you have any triggers please head over to my website for a full list of content warnings:

# CHAPTER ONE

Sasha

SWEAT DRIPS down my back as Carter holds eye contact with me. We both struggle to catch full breaths, and my heart races a mile a minute. I feel almost high right now, something I always experience when I'm dancing.

I've been dancing since I was five years old when my mother enrolled me in a ballet class to help with my clumsiness. I don't think there has been a single day since then that I haven't danced. It's in my blood now, and I don't think there would be any way to get it out. It's who I am, and even if I'm not doing it professionally, I'd never give it up.

The music ends, and I clap my hands, beaming at my student.

"You killed it today. You clearly didn't slack off over the summer," I praise him, resulting in the top of his ears brightening to a deep shade of red. He's always so adorable when he blushes. "If you ever wanted to give up basketball and become a dancer, you could do it in a heartbeat."

He chuckles, grabbing his towel to wipe off his face, trailing down to dry his chest and fantastic abs. I might have put Carter strictly in the do-not-touch box because he's my dance student and was only eighteen when I first met him, but that doesn't mean I can't appreciate how gorgeous he is. He's tall as fuck, like most basketball players, and has a lean build with muscles in all the right places. His jet-black hair, rich brown skin, and alluring chestnut eyes tie the whole package together. I internally fan myself. Whoever gets to take that man home is one lucky son of a bitch.

"If dance paid as good as the NBA is supposed to, I'd consider it but we both know it doesn't," he replies, and I sigh.

"You're preaching to the choir. Why do you think I'm in law school and not dancing full time? I need something to pay the bills."

"Do you not like law school?" he asked, seemingly genuinely interested.

I shake my head. "I do, but obviously, dance is my main passion."

Carter nods like he understands. "I love basketball and dance equally, which makes things easier. If something happens and I don't get drafted to the NBA, maybe I'll try to dance professionally."

An alarm goes off on my phone and Carter packs his stuff up, knowing my next students will be arriving soon.

"I'll see you next week," he tells me, waving as he walks out the door.

I take a moment to check out his perfect ass as he leaves because even though I've friend zoned him, I still can appreciate the view. He pauses just outside and turns to wink at me.

"You'd think after all this time you'd be over checking my ass out," he teases.

"I will never get sick of an ass like that," I retort, making him laugh as he walks down the hall.

Once he's gone, I get busy setting up for my class of little ballet dancers.

Green Spring Dance Academy pays me well for the classes I teach and only takes a small percentage of what I charge private students, like Carter, to cover the facility fees. But it barely covers my bills. Once I have to start paying back my student loans, it won't be enough. Even if I worked here full time, it wouldn't cut it. Besides, *teaching* dance was never my dream. I wanted to be the center of attention, on stage every night, dancing in front of a sold-out audience. Unfortunately, most people's dreams never come true. Mine were ripped away by a man I thought I loved. I've come to terms with the fact that I'll never dance professionally, but at least I get to keep dance in my life this way.

As I'm placing the little mats on the floor for my students to sit on, giggles and chatting fill the hall, alerting me that at least a few of my students are here already. I'm unable to fight the giant grin that spreads across my lips at the sound of their joyous noises. Teaching preschoolers is not an easy feat, but these kiddos have quickly stolen my heart. Especially the sole boy in my class, Andy. He's an absolute gem. His head is always held high, and he sashays around the room like it's his life's duty. The way he answers questions with such sass reminds me of a younger me. I hope he never loses his sparkle. I know from experience how empty it makes you when someone tries to take that away from you.

An eerie shudder creeps up my spine as memories of my past try to open the door I barricaded when I moved to Green Spring, Michigan. It's not often that my brain takes me back to those dark days, but when it does, it throws me for a loop. I've worked so hard to try and forget about the life I left behind, but there are still times that the memories try to rear their ugly head and make me feel small again. I struggle to take in a few deep breaths, but eventually, I'm able to even my breathing out. I give my head a quick shake, shoving the thoughts away. The past is always better left there. I have an amazing life now, and nothing good would come from going back there, even in my head.

After taking a deep inhale through my nose and blowing it out slowly through my mouth, I straighten my messy bun on the top of my head and plaster on my smile before heading towards the door to let my students in. Hopefully, those memories won't try to make an appearance again for a long time.

"Hello, my beautiful angels," I greet the children. "Who's ready to dance their hearts out?"

A bunch of hands rise into the air then they quickly scurry into the classroom. Andy sashaying his way to his mat, like he always does, making my smile grow even wider. Man, I love that kid.

ALL OF MY classes fly by quickly like they usually do. By the time I've put everything away, I'm beyond exhausted, but that doesn't stop me from grinning from ear to ear. I love my job. Seeing my students grow and succeed is just the icing on the cake.

"Fuck!" Lyla, another teacher, shrieks from down the hall, causing alarm bells to go off in my head.

Without thinking twice, I race toward her, running as fast as my feet will take me. When I enter her room, I gasp at the amount of water pouring from the ceiling directly onto Lyla.

"What the hell happened?" I ask Lyla, her clothes are soaking wet and her eyes are glassy with unshed tears.

"I-I-I don't know," she stammers while shaking. "I noticed some water on the floor and was cleaning it up when the ceiling opened and started raining on me."

Her teeth chatter, but she doesn't move. She must be in shock, so I step forward, grab her hand, and pull her out of the stream.

"I've got a change of clothes that might fit you," I tell her, dragging her to my room. "I'll call Shelly to let her know that something is leaking."

Lyla nods, trembling from being so cold.

"Do you need me to call an ambulance?" I check, worry creeping its way up and how badly my friend is trembling.

"I think I'll be okay as soon as I get out of these wet clothes," she assures me.

I stare at her for a moment, trying to decide if I believe her or not, but besides the shivers, she doesn't look too bad. I'll just make sure to keep an eye on her after she's changed.

Once I've given her my clothes, I grab my phone and call our boss Shelly.

"Is everything okay?" Shelly answers, confusion evident in her voice since I never call her at this hour.

"I'm sorry, but it's not. Do you know where the building's water shutoff is? The ceiling in the red room is pouring water, but we don't know why. Lyla is changing right now; she got soaked when the ceiling opened above her."

"Was she hurt?" Shelly asks with a concerned tone.

"I don't think so, just shaken up by being drenched in freezing water."

"Shit," Shelly curses under her breath. "I don't think you'll be able to access the water shut off. I'm on my way. I'll call Mack on the drive. If anything else happens, please let me know."

"You've got it," I assure her as Lyla reenters the room.

"I can't believe that happened," she grumbles, "you'd think there would have been more than a small puddle of water before the ceiling started pouring like that."

"It was the corner of the room where the storage area is. Maybe the majority of water is under the shelves, and you couldn't see it."

Lyla hums her agreement. "Wait, isn't there an old guy who lives above the dance studio? Do you think he's okay?"

Shit I had completely forgotten about the man who lives upstairs. Picking my phone up again I re-dial Shelly's number.

"What now?" she answers.

"Lyla reminded me of the old guy who lives above the studio. Should we call the cops to make sure he's okay?"

"Mack told me Abel is out of town this week so he should be fine," she assures me. "But Mack's on his way as well and has keys to the apartment, so he'll check it out."

I relay the information to Lyla, who instantly relaxes as we wait for our boss and the owner of the building to arrive.

Mack and Shelly show up within minutes of each other, and Mack shuts the water off before heading upstairs to check on the apartment.

Shelly gasps when we enter the red room and even I'm caught off guard at the sight. There is so much more water than the last time Lyla and I were in here. "Holy shit," she whispers before walking out of the room with me and Lyla on her heels. "It's late. There's nothing more you can do, so head home, and I'll call you both in the morning."

"Are you sure you don't want help cleaning up?' Lyla asks.

Shelly shakes her head. "We'll figure out everything tomorrow."

"This fucking sucks," I murmur as we walk out of the building.

"It's going to be fine," Lyla tells me, then nibbles on her lower lip. "Isn't it?"

"You saw how much damage there was, Lyla. There's a strong possibility the studio will be forced to shut down for a while."

She pouts. "Fuck."

"You can say that twice."

"I guess it's time to start job hunting again," she says with a sigh.

I nod, then give her a hug, wishing her all the best before heading in the opposite direction to my house.

I can't believe this is happening. It's just my fucking luck.

But I don't have time to let panic set in. I have to come up with a gameplan, and fast.

This isn't the first time I've had to pivot and come up with a new plan, and it most likely won't be the last. Unfortunately, I don't have any money to fall back on this time, but I won't let that derail me. I'm so close to having my dreams come true and I'll do anything to make that happen. I've never let anything keep me down and I sure as hell won't let this stop me. I'm a fighter and will handle anything the universe throws at me. I just kind of wish I didn't have to keep fighting all the time.

# CHAPTER TWO

MY EYES ARE TRAINED on the ball as I race toward my opponent, who is currently dribbling it down the pitch toward our net. With a swift kick, I steal the ball and then immediately pass it to BooBoo with a precision I've become known for over the last four years of playing for the Green Spring Koala's soccer team. When I send a ball, it always goes exactly where I want it to. Unless someone intercepts it, of course. I've trained extremely hard to home in my aiming skills and become as good as I am. I very rarely am off these days, which makes everyone on the team happy.

BooBoo dribbles the ball across the field before passing it to Whiley, who scores us another goal seconds before the timer runs out.

"That's how it's done!" Whiley shouts as our entire team rushes toward him to celebrate the win.

We cheer, high-five, and bro hug before heading off the field for a briefing with our coach.

"Great job, boys," Coach starts his speech when we are all gathered. "But we need to keep up the hard work. The season has only just begun, and I love the drive everyone already has, but we have a long road ahead of us. As much as we need you to continue to hone your skills and keep your bodies in peak condition, you also have to make sure your grades are up. The last thing we need as a team is to be dropping players because your priorities aren't straight. I want all of you to have balanced lives, but if you want to bring home the championship win, your focus needs to be almost solely on school and soccer for the next three-ish months."

I nod along to Coach's words. Soccer has been my life since I was a child. Even when I was six years old, I gave it everything I had. Maybe that's because the coaches on my team actually paid attention to me, unlike my parents.

I know how to prioritize my life to make sure I give my all to the sport. I haven't been able to bring home a championship win since I started at Green Spring University, and this is my last year to do it. I've been so close so many times I could almost taste it. I don't want it to fall through my fingers once again.

After coach gives us the go-ahead, we rush to the showers to get ourselves clean and changed so we can go home and study. Such is the life of a college athlete.

Some athletes have dreams of going pro, and while I thought that was the road I wanted to take when I first got to GSU, I've since changed my mind. To be honest, I'm not the best athlete out there, and my chances of going pro aren't as good as some. I'm a good college soccer player, but there's a difference between playing for a college team and going pro. But I had no idea what I wanted to do outside of soccer. When I started classes, I was still uncertain about what major I would take until I met with an advisor and found my love for teaching. It was like an ah-ha moment for me, and everything fell into place. When I graduate in the summer, I'm hoping to get a job at a high school as a gym teacher. I'll be able to stay active but also guide young minds. Maybe I'll even have the opportunity to coach a soccer team, which would make me beyond happy. I'd get to pass on all the knowledge I've learned over my years of playing.

I should start figuring out where I'm going to live when I graduate, but I don't want to think about that right now.

Maybe I'll put more thought into it after the soccer season is over. I guess I could go home, but I don't really want to do that. All that's waiting for me there are parents who couldn't give a shit about me and people I'd rather not see again. Which means I'm kind of a free agent and can go where my heart takes me. I just don't have the slightest clue as to where that is at this moment.

Once I'm changed, I say goodbye to my teammates and make the short drive home to the apartment I share with my friends.

The radio is tuned to an oldies station playing a familiar tune as I travel down the road. I tap my fingers on the steering wheel and hum along to the song. The traffic isn't bad tonight, but I honestly never mind if it takes me a bit longer to get home. I enjoy the time alone, jamming to some music, and forgetting everything else. Ever since I got my driver's license at sixteen, I've always loved going for long drives to clear my mind. I'm pretty sure I got that love from my grandfather. He was the type of person to randomly go on a road trip just because.

A sense of longing fills my chest as my thoughts drift to my granddad. The summer he took me on a month-long road trip pops into my head, and a soft smile spreads across my lips. So many things went wrong on that vacation, but there wasn't a day that I was sad. He taught me to take the lemons life gives you and turn them into lemonade. My grandad was more of a parent than my actual parents. I spent any free time I had with him. He would come to all of my soccer games, and he was my biggest supporter. Even when I told him that I thought I liked boys and girls he didn't bat an eye. He simply told me love is love and it didn't matter who I was attracted to as long as they treated me well.

He was the best man I ever met, and when he passed away when I was twelve, it hit me harder than I thought it would. After he died, I felt more alone than I ever had. My parents weren't abusive, but they didn't care, and that didn't change after his passing. So, to say I was excited to leave that shit town and move to Green Spring, Michigan, would be an understatement.

I take a deep breath and hold it for a moment before slowly blowing it out. "I love you, PopPop," I whisper, hoping that wherever he is, he can hear me.

"THERE'S THE MVP," Monster says when I open the door to our apartment.

I shake my head but that doesn't stop a smile from spreading across my face. I love that my friends were free to come to my game tonight and witness our team kill it. I'll do the same for Monster when baseball season starts. I would also do the same for our other roommate, Bronny, when his wrestling season begins, but he's got a superstition about his friends watching him, so we respect that and don't attend any of his matches.

I head straight to my room to drop my bag off and grab my textbook before joining my roommates in the living room, plopping onto the couch when I arrive.

"How's studying?" I ask as I situate the pillows and get more comfortable.

Both Monster and Bronny are in the large comfortable recliners that are on either side of the living room. Monster has a pencil behind his ear, which pushes back some of his shaggy brown hair that is covering his forehead and poking into his eyes a little, but it doesn't seem to bother him.

Bronny has a book in his lap and shrugs. "About as good as it normally goes," he responds, groaning a little bit.

I chuckle. "Yeah, a part of me is excited to be finished with all the studying when I graduate."

"But the other part is scared shitless that you're going to be thrown into the real world and have to get a job?" Monster checks, making me laugh.

"That about sums it up."

"Hopefully, I'll get signed by the MLB and won't have to worry too much," he has this dreamy look on his face that he always gets when he starts thinking about playing professionally.

"I don't think I'll mind working for a living, but I'm not sure how I'll feel about living on my own," Bronny adds.

"Yeah, that's going to take some getting used to for sure," Monster replies.

"My parents weren't around a lot when I was growing up. It kind of felt like I was living on my own when I was a teenager, so I don't think I'll mind it too much, but I'll probably miss you losers," I supply.

There's still a smile on my face as I talk with my friends, but bringing up my parents leaves a bitter taste in my mouth. When I was young, I went to my grandpa's house after school, or they would hire a sitter to watch me when they went off to get drunk or whatever they did, but when I turned twelve, and grandpa passed away, it was up to me to take care of my myself. I was in charge of feeding myself, making my own lunches, and tucking myself into bed at night. If I needed help with homework, I went to my friends. It was lonely at times, but my friends were amazing and loved me more than my parents ever did.

"Even when we aren't living together anymore, we'll still be friends. I'll make sure to harass you as much as possible," Monster assures me with a toothy grin.

"Aww, you're going to remember us small fries when you're a super famous baseball player?" I tease him.

"Like they say, never forget where you come from."

I'd like to forget where I came from, or at least the people that I came from, but I get what he's saying and appreciate that he'll want to continue our friendship. I'm not afraid that he won't follow through because I already have one friend who became a professional athlete. We still talk on the phone at least once a month and text each other constantly. Chase will always be one of my best friends.

My phone buzzes in my pocket, and I almost snicker when I figure out who's texting me. It's almost like he knew I was thinking about him.

Chase: Killer game! Way to start out the season strong.

Me: Thanks! Our team is meshing super well. Hopefully we will keep that up.

Chase: You've got this!

Me: Thanks man. You guys have killed it in the preseason. Are you excited for the regular season to start?

Chase: Yes! I'm ready to bring home another Super Bowl win.

I chuckle because even though I'm only reading his words, I can practically *feel* his excitement. Chase is a man who lives, breathes, and eats football. His only other love is his family and his husband. How he ended up snagging a nerdy lawyer who hated all sports when they first met still baffles me some days, but I'm happy for them. I'd like to find the kind of love they have one day. Unfortunately, that's easier said than done.

Dating in college isn't easy when you're demisexual. Most people aren't actually looking to build a relationship they only want to fuck, and I'm not sexually attracted to anyone until I've developed a close relationship with them. It's crazy how small the circle is on dating apps when sex is completely off the table. I've had a few people *try*, but very few stick it out for long. I'm usually left with the *you're a nice guy, but this isn't working out* line.

In high school, I had a couple of relationships and lost my virginity, but nothing lasted for long. It took me a while to come to terms with actually being demi, accepting myself for who I am, and getting over feeling like I was broken. Growing up and maturing helped a lot with that. It is hard to do that when you are younger because being different can feel like the worst thing.

I know now that things aren't going to happen for me the same as they do for others, and that's okay.

I don't mind being single because my focus should be on soccer and finishing college, but eventually, I'd like to find someone to settle down with.

While I think about a future with a partner by my side, an overly flamboyant flirt with forest green eyes, long flowy blonde locks, and a jawline so perfect he must have been blessed by some form of deity pops into my head, and it causes me to pause.

Why the hell am I thinking about Sasha of all people? A man who I only met because his best friend was dating my best friend. Then he just decided that he was going to stay in my life even after they left. A guy who is ridiculously pushy and tiptoes on my boundary line at any given chance. Someone I've only *just* started to think of as a friend. A person who most definitely would *not* make a good life partner. Quickly I push away the insane thoughts and try to focus on my studies. The last thing I need right now is to develop feelings for the biggest player I know.

But of course forgetting about Sasha is easier said than done when he bursts through the front door seconds later, like my thoughts summoned him or something.

It doesn't take me long to realize something is off as Sasha makes his way toward us. His normally well-groomed hair is a mess, looking almost matted in places like he slept on it wrong or he's been running his fingers through it so much that it got bunched up. His eyes are bloodshot, and tear stains mark his beautiful face, causing my heart to ache for him. What the hell happened?

"You look like shit," Monster notes.

"I've had a couple of really shitty days," he confesses, his bottom lip wobbling a bit like he's going to cry again. "Max isn't home, and I just don't want to be alone right now."

Max is Sasha's roommate and one of his best friends and who he would normally go to when shit went sideways, but it makes sense that our place would be his backup plan. For some reason, he decided after meeting us that we should all be best friends. Monster and Bronny were one hundred percent on board from the get-go, but I was a bit more apprehensive. His persistent flirting annoyed the shit out of me and had me judging him before I really got to know him. I have always tried to hold my judgments on people until I've had a chance to spend more time with them, but I didn't do that with Sasha. I immediately put him in the annoying acquaintance category without giving him a chance to show me who he really is.

That didn't stop Sasha from showing up all of the time and inserting himself into my life, whether I liked it or not. Eventually I learned that my assumptions about him were all wrong, but I was also too embarrassed to admit that to him, so I've kept up my nonchalant behavior around him. Acting like he still annoys the shit out of me, when in reality, that isn't the case. Although how I *actually* feel about him is still unclear to me.

But judging by how I have the urge to wrap him in my arms right now and wipe away his tears, he means more to me than I thought. Of course, I don't do that. Instead, I sit up to give Sasha a place to sit on the couch with me and don't say a word.

"What happened?" Bronny asks, closing his book and leaning forward to give Sasha his full attention.

Sasha takes a shaky breath as he takes his spot beside me. Again, I want to hold him, to push away his sadness and give him the strength he needs. But that would be way out of the ordinary for me, so I keep my hands to myself.

"There was a water leak at the dance studio the other night, and the owner called me last night to inform me that the building is going to take six months to remodel. I have no idea what I'm going to do. It's not like I can go that long without a job."

"The studio can't change locations in the meantime?" Monster inquires.

Sasha sighs while shaking his head. "Apparently, there is nothing available that would fit their needs."

"I can take you job hunting if you'd like," Monster offers, bringing a small smile to Sasha's lips.

"I appreciate that, but I don't want to be a bother," he replies, but Monster shakes his head.

"I promise it wouldn't be a bother. Friends help friends," Monster states, and a glimmer of hope shines in Sasha's eyes.

"Thank you," he whispers.

"I'll help too if you want," I tell Sasha without fully thinking it through, which obviously shocks him just as much and causes his brows to shoot up.

"Really?" he questions doubtfully.

I shrug trying to act how I normally do around him. "I mean, as long as I'm not busy," I add on.

Sasha studies me for a moment, clearly unsure of how to react, but eventually, he shrugs and accepts my offer. "The more help, the better, I suppose."

"Did you want to crash on our couch tonight so you don't

have to be alone?" I suggest next, and Sasha looks at me like I've grown a second head.

"You really have to stop acting nice, or I'm going to have to call the FBI and report that you've been body snatched," he jokes, finally starting to sound like his old self again.

I roll my eyes while suppressing a smile. "Ugh, you do one nice thing for a guy, and he acts like it's such a big deal. Guess I won't be doing that again anytime soon."

"Ahh there's the Rio I know and love," he teases, bumping his shoulder into mine. "But if the offer is genuine, I would like to crash here tonight. It just feels like the world is collapsing around me, and being alone sounds miserable."

"Even if Rio wasn't being serious, you can totally crash here," Monster tells him and I don't bother arguing that I'm not always a sarcastic ass because I mostly have been when it comes to Sasha, so I see why they would think that way.

"I don't care either way," I say and start to collect my things. "But I'm going to bed, so I'll see everyone in the morning."

My roommates and Sasha tell me goodnight as I make my way to my room to be alone with my thoughts.

It's confusing as hell that I'm suddenly drawn to Sasha like this, but I don't think there is anything I can do about it. Maybe these feelings will pass soon, and everything can go back to how it was.

Here's hoping, anyway.

# CHAPTER THREE

MY FEET DRAG across the tiles as I shuffle my way to class. This past week has been an absolute shit show.

I spent the entire weekend job hunting with Monster and Rio, but unfortunately, nothing caught my interest. I know beggars can't be choosers, but the hours for most of the places hiring are horrible, and they pay pennies. Unfortunately, if I want to continue to have a roof over my head and put food in my belly, I have to find something as soon as possible.

Spending the weekend with Rio was confusing and awkward. Normally, he acts like he'd rather not be around me, although he never actually leaves, even when he can. But the past two days, he was acting differently. Not a lot, but enough to weird me out.

I've had a crush on him since I first met him. But I always thought I was just an annoyance to him, so I didn't do more than flirt and push his buttons when I could. I knew there was no chance of him liking me back, at least that's what I assumed, but things felt different this weekend. But there are more pressing matters to worry about at the moment, so I try to push the ridiculously hot soccer player out of my mind.

"Hey, Sasha," Carter shouts out, pulling me from my thoughts. I pause, turning to find him racing down the hall toward me.

"Hey, handsome, how's it going?" I ask, tucking a lock of hair behind my ear.

"It's going," he replies with a shrug. "But I've got a proposition for you."

I place my hand on his shoulder and sigh. "You're hot as sin, but I've already told you we're better off friends."

Carter throws his head back, laughing. "Not that, you idiot. But if I did swing that way, I would totally be begging you to date me," he jokes with a wink. "I was just meeting with my coach and overheard the Director of Spirit Programs and Events say they need a new mascot. I guess one of the guys who has been doing it for the last three years got arrested. She was upset because she didn't want to hold a whole new audition process. I told her I knew the perfect candidate, and she said you could meet with her this evening. I hope that was okay. I assumed you had time since this is normally when our dance session is, but obviously, we canceled it this week."

"You want me to be a mascot?" I question, my eyebrows jumping up to the top of my forehead.

"You need the job, don't you?" he retorts. "I have no idea what the position pays, but it's something. Plus, you'd get to dance and have a good time."

I press my lips together, processing what he's telling me. I don't see the harm in at least talking to the director. The worst that could happen would be it's not the right fit for me. The best would be that it hopefully pays well, and I enjoy doing it. This is my last year at GSU, so it's not like I'd have to do this forever.

"Did she say when and where to meet her?" I ask, making Carter's face light up.

"Six o'clock in her office," he tells me. "I can take you there if you want."

I smile at him and nod. "That would be great."

"Cool. I'll meet you at the east wing entrance at five forty-five," he says before heading off to his next class.

I stare at the back of his head as he walks away. I guess I'm going for an interview tonight.

MY PALMS ARE SWEATING, and it feels like I have a live wire coursing through my body as I follow Carter down the hall to the Director of Spirit Programs and Events office. I haven't interviewed for anything in a long time, and I'm hella nervous. What if this lady doesn't like me, or what if she doesn't think I'm the right fit for the job? The only thing that's stopping me from full-on hyperventilating is the knowledge that I actually have experience being a mascot. The dance academy puts on a carnival every year and I've been tasked with donning the unicorn costume each time. Mostly, my job is just to stand around and greet the children, but I also do a dance routine that has the children laughing and cheering every time. But that still doesn't mean I'm cut out for the job of a full-time mascot.

When I first started at GSU, I considered auditioning for the school mascot. But at the time, I was trying to keep a low profile. All I wanted to do was keep my head down and do the work I needed to do. Obviously, no one would know it was me in the costume, but I still didn't want the attention. I was very much in my hiding phase I was afraid of someone from my past finding me, and that would have been detrimental. After a year of living in the shadows, I was sick of suppressing myself. I wanted to be the guy I used to be. The one who loved to laugh, be over the top, and not give a fuck what people said. Since the man I was hiding from hadn't shown up in a year, I figured it was safe to finally start living my actual life.

Now that I'm unapologetically myself, I'm not afraid to be the center of attention. In fact, I crave it. Hopefully, my over-the-top personality and talent will be enough to convince this lady to give me a chance.

"Want me to wait for you?" Carter checks once we've arrived at the office.

I wave him off. "Nah. Who knows how long this is going to take. But I do appreciate you showing me the way. I've never been on this side of campus before."

Carter smiles, his pretty chestnut eyes lighting up in the process. "Not a problem, I'll see you around. Hopefully, we can figure out a place to continue our dance lessons soon."

He nods and then heads in the opposite direction of me. I stare at the door for a moment, taking a deep breath before finally gaining the courage to knock.

"Come in," a female voice calls out. She sounds tired, and I pray she's in a good mood, or at the very least, a hiring mood. I need this job.

"Hi, I'm Sasha Lawrence. Carter told me you'd be expecting me," I say as I enter the office.

The woman smiles at me, and even though there are dark circles under her pale blue eyes, they seem warm and inviting. "Yes, I'm Evangeline, Director of Spirit Programs and Events. It's nice to meet you. Please have a seat."

I take the seat across from her desk and then wait patiently for her to continue.

"Thank you for coming to talk to me. Carter told me you're a dancer with mascot experience," she checks, looking up from her sheet and eyeing me.

"Yes. I've donned the unicorn costume at the Green Spring Dance Academy summer festival for the last five years. Obviously, that is only one day a year, but I know I can handle the mascot costume. I've been dancing my entire life and am strong enough to maneuver the outfit with ease. I can show you one of the routines I've done in the past if you like."

"That would be wonderful," she tells me with the same warm smile on her face.

I quickly pull up the video of my routine from this summer's festival then pass my phone over to Evangeline.

She watches the video of me doing a flawless routine full of flips, cartwheels and dancing before handing it back to me.

"You're extremely talented," she starts, and I can't help but preen a little from her praise. "I'll admit this isn't how we normally do things. Usually, a tryout is held, and we have people audition for at least a full day, but time isn't on our side right now. We already held tryouts the week before school started and picked a team we thought was solid. With the loss of one of our team members, we are scrambling to find a replacement. We already went through the list of people who were in the top spots but didn't make the cut and have had zero luck finding someone to take the position. Everyone already has commitments that make it impossible for them to take on the role."

"That sounds intense," I respond sympathetically. "But depending on what the position pays, I could definitely help you out. I recently lost my job at the Green Spring Dance Academy due to a flood, so my schedule is wide open."

"All of our mascot team members receive fair compensation as we know it's a fairly heavy time commitment," she assures me before sliding a piece of paper in front of me.

I quickly scan the contract, smiling at the rate that's being offered. It's a bit less than what the dance academy paid me, but the access to the athletic center means I'll no longer need a gym membership.

"There are some strict rules to being a mascot that you'll have to adhere to. They are outlined at the bottom, but they probably aren't much different than what you had to do with the dance academy," Evangeline explains.

I move my head up and down as I read the rules. It's pretty much all the normal stuff for mascots, like rules that prohibit talking, removing the head, or breaking character in front of crowds, but there is also a mandatory grade average I'll have to keep, which won't be a problem for me.

"None of this will be a problem for me," I promise her. "Does that mean I got the job?"

She chuckles and shrugs. "I don't see why not. The first month will be extremely intense for you as you'll have to learn all of the group routines with the cheer squad, as well as creating a few original solo routines. You'll also be shadowed for the first couple of weeks to make sure you're a good fit for the job. Does that all sound okay for you?"

"Absolutely," I respond quickly. "I know I can do this."

She smiles then reaches across her desk. "Welcome to the team."

I shake her hand, thanking her for the opportunity before taking the contract home with me to more thoroughly go over before I sign it.

When this school year started, I had no idea I was going to be a koala mascot, but here we are. Let's just pray I don't fuck this up.

# CHAPTER FOUR

SWEAT DRIPS down my back causing my jersey to stick to my torso as I dribble the ball across the pitch, passing to a team mate as soon as they're open. Once the ball is in their possession, they fire it at the net and earn us another point.

Cheerleaders and our giant koala mascot, Kerrington, get the crowd going with a chant as our team gets back into position. I'm subbed out for a couple of minutes to get a drink and to calm my racing heart.

"Is that a new mascot?" I ask BooBoo, who's sitting on the bench with me.

Whoever is in the mascot costume today seems more energetic than they normally are, but maybe they had more energy drinks today.

"I think so. Brent got arrested last week, and they needed to replace him. Evangeline is here and she only hangs around when newbies are being trained," he points out, and I lean forward to get a better look at the mascot and cheer squad.

Just like BooBoo said, Evangeline is standing with the cheer coach watching the Koala intently.

"Any word on who the rookie is?" I ask.

"Nope and I didn't see them getting ready either," he informs me.

The mascots have their own changing area since a few of the people are girls and it wouldn't be right for them to have to share our locker room. While the identity of who is inside Kerrington the Koala isn't general public knowledge, all the athletes at GSU are usually friendly with the mascot team.

I return my attention to the pitch just in time to witness our team score again. I stand up and cheer before glancing back at the sidelines to see the Koala do a backflip in celebration. We don't always have the mascot at our games like the football team does, but when we do, it's always entertaining. Whoever the new mascot member is, they are a ball of energy.

Coach signals that it's my turn to get back in the game and like I always do, I put all my focus on the task at hand.

With a giant smile on my face, I get into position. I love soccer so much that it almost sucks this is my last season playing at a level like this. Nothing ever brought me the kind of joy soccer does. I was worried about losing my passion once I graduate, but thankfully, I have teaching to look forward to now.

I move my body weight from foot to foot, scanning the pitch, waiting for the ball to get in motion and for the play to start. The outside world, the cheers from the crowd, looming graduation, where I'm going to live, and everything that has been taking up space in my brain begins to fade away, and all I see is the here and now on this field. Nothing else matters at this moment.

Once the ball is moving, I spring into motion while my teammate steals the ball and dribbles it down the pitch toward our opponent's net. I stay close, trying to make sure no one steals the ball.

It doesn't take long for an opponent to steal the ball, but I'm ready for him, pumping my legs as hard as they will go. The smell of sweat and turf fills my nostrils as I breathe in deeply. A cocky smirk spreads across my lips as I run straight toward my opponent and, at the last second, twist and kick the ball through his feet before racing around him to dribble the ball back in the direction we were heading moments ago.

With my focus so intently on the game, I didn't notice the clock ticking down, and when the crowd starts counting down, I know it's now or never to score the last goal of the game. Even though I'm not as close as I'd like to be, I have a clear path to the net, so I draw my leg back, using all my power to send the ball sailing. I keep my eyes on the ball, holding my breath until it lands in the net. At the goal I throw my hands up, celebrating the perfect shot. The crowd roars loudly; it's almost deafening, but it has me grinning from ear to ear.

"What a fucking shot!" BooBoo shouts, bumping his shoulder into mine.

I shoot him a cocky smile, but my attention is quickly pulled from my friend to the overly energetic Koala, who is now on the main field celebrating our win with the cheerleaders and the rest of the team. After a few backflips, the mascot makes his way over to me, lifting my arm like I won a wrestling match or something. My natural instinct is to pull away, but the fans begin to cheer even louder, obviously loving the interaction, so I play along, throwing my other arm up too.

"Don't steal all the glory, hotshot. It was a team effort," Whiley teases, and I wrap my free arm around his shoulder.

"Aww, is someone feeling left out?" I joke back, laughing when he sticks his tongue out at me.

Kerrington eventually drops my arm, going back to join the cheerleaders for another dance routine. I wonder who is under the mask. The mysterious new mascot seems to be holding the crowd's attention much better than normal. I can't help but stare at him, but I have no idea why. I've never paid much attention to the giant koala before, so why is it holding my attention today?

After celebrating on the field, I head to the locker room with my team to have our debriefing with Coach. Thankfully, I stop thinking about the koala, that is until I'm walking down the hall and hear singing coming from the mascot changing room. An alluring baritone voice flutters out the door, causing my feet to stop and take in the beautiful singing.

"Kerrington can dance *and* sing," BooBoo notes, startling me which makes my heart race.

"When did you start walking so quietly?" I chastise him and he has the audacity to laugh.

"I didn't, your head was just too far in the clouds as you got lost in the voice of our new Koala," he replies.

I roll my eyes. "I'm tired. It has nothing to do with the new mascot."

BooBoo pats me on the shoulder. "Sure thing." His tone tells me he doesn't actually believe me, but I'm not going to stand here and argue with him further.

"Are you going to Whiley's party?" I ask, walking away from the hypnotizing voice of the new mascot, whoever they are.

"Obviously," BooBoo tells me with a toothy grin. "What kind of party animal would I be if I stayed home?"

I chuckle. BooBoo got his nickname at a party his first weekend at GSU last year. He was beyond drunk, even though he was only eighteen, but that isn't abnormal at a college party. He smashed his leg into a coffee table and immediately fell to the ground, clutching the limb to his chest, asking everyone around him to kiss his booboo better. The nickname stuck instantly. I'm pretty sure he'll never live it down, but that doesn't seem to upset him. In fact, I'm pretty sure he secretly loves the nickname because it's so unique. A lot better than Robert Hetterton, his real name. It's also much better than how I got my nickname, but no one really knows that story anymore, and that makes me happy.

"Make sure to keep it tame," I remind him like I do every time there's a party. "You're still underage. The last thing we need is you getting benched because you were being an idiot."

BooBoo is one of our best players. It would totally fuck things up if he couldn't play.

"Yes, Dad," he grumbles.

I get that being young sucks, and he just wants to fit in, but you don't need to get drunk to do that. At least, I never did. But I'm not him, and I don't know what it's like inside his head, so I keep my mouth shut. We've already had a conversation about him staying sober, so if he wants to risk it, it's up to him.

"Are you coming?" he checks, and I shake my head.

"My roommates planned a movie night to help cheer up, Sasha, who hasn't had the best of luck the past couple of weeks," I explain.

He nods in understanding. "It's good to have your friend's backs when you can."

When we get to the parking lot, we head in opposite directions, and I don't take any detours on my way home, hoping I'm not the last person to arrive.

"Sasha here yet?" I check when I enter the apartment.

"Not yet," Monster informs me. "Apparently, he landed himself a new job, but he won't tell me what it is." He pauses with furrowed brows. "You don't think he's stripping, do you?"

"Would it be a problem if he was?" I check, tilting my head to the side.

Monster presses his lips together obviously thinking it over before shaking his head. "I guess not. I just don't want to see him getting hurt. He's a good guy."

I smile at how caring my giant friend is. You'd think that a man his size would be an intimidating menace, but he's totally a softy.

"Sasha can take care of himself," I remind him.

"I'm aware of that, but I also have gotten to know Sasha

pretty well over the last year, and he doesn't always think things through. What if he started stripping because he knows he's an amazing dancer but didn't think about the clientele he would be serving?"

"Maybe he got hired at the high-end 2SLGBTQIA+ night club on the outskirts of town. It's a members only club, and they do intensive background checks. At least, that's what I heard. Also, everyone that works there has to sign NDAs. Maybe that's why he can't talk about it," I supply, not really thinking that Sasha got a job as a stripper, but if he did, Waterfalls would definitely be a place suited for him.

"Isn't that a sex club?" Monster questions, and I laugh at how wide his eyes have gotten.

"Yes, but that's not all it is. You can just go there to dance and have a good time like any nightclub, or you can take in a strip tease on one of the stages. There's also areas where people put on full nudity shows if you know what I'm saying," I tell him and wink at the end.

He gasps. "You mean people have sex on stage?"

"Yes, and others masturbate to it in the audience," I add. "But if you don't want to participate in something like that, you don't have to. All the areas of the club are separate."

"Why did you sign up for a club like that if you're demisexual?" he asks without any judgment in his tone, just pure curiosity.

"Just because I don't want to have sex with someone I haven't developed a close connection with doesn't mean I don't want to dance and have a good time. I've actually had some of the best nights there because the club provides special bracelets to symbolize a bunch of different things. I wear one that broadcasts I'm demi and not looking to hook up. People respect that and I'm able to let loose without the fear that someone is going to try and pressure me into something I'm not comfortable with. The club is *huge* on consent, and if anyone goes against the rules, they get banned."

Monster is silent for a moment as he takes in what I just said. "That sounds really cool. Do you think you could help me become a member? I'd like to check it out."

"When you're twenty-one, I'll be happy to help you," I tell him, and he sighs.

"Being young sucks," he grumbles.

"Getting old is worse," Sasha tells him, and I quickly turn to see the vibrant twink entering our apartment.

"Haven't you ever heard of knocking?" I check with a raised brow.

He waves me off while closing the door behind him. "Why would I have to do such a thing? This is practically my second home."

Sasha has been spending a lot of time at our apartment, and I'll admit that he's been growing on me over the past year, but I'll never let him know that. As far as he knows, his mere presence annoys me, and I just put up with him. And to be honest that was true for a long time. He was too over the top for my liking, and I just thought he was a playboy who didn't care about anything. As I got to know him better, I realized that wasn't true, but at the same time, I kept up my charade of not caring about him. I'll never tell him that I admire his sweet and caring side. The way he takes care of his neighbors who can't take care of themselves, like mowing their lawns or tending to their gardens, with no expectation of getting anything in return. I've started to see under his over-the-top personality to the person he really is, which is a good guy.

"That's weird. I haven't seen your name on the rental agreement," I tell him, keeping up the charade.

Sasha rolls his eyes, then pulls Monster in for a hug. "Why are you wanting to grow up so fast?"

Monster's cheeks turn an adorable shade of pink, and he shrugs. "No reason," he mumbles.

"We were talking about Waterfalls," I inform Sasha, and his eyes light up with a mischievous joy.

"I love that place," he gushes. "I was really hoping they would be hiring when the dance academy got flooded, but unfortunately, they weren't."

"So your new job isn't a stripper?" Monster blurts out.

Sasha throws his head back, letting out a hearty laugh that wraps its way around me, caressing me like a lover would. Goosebumps erupt over my arms, and my cock stirs the tiniest amount. I almost gasp at the sudden feeling. Since when have I ever reacted this way to someone's laugh?

Sasha sighs at Monster, thankfully not paying me any attention. My face is suddenly hot and probably a bright shade of red, so I quickly head down the hall, making a beeline for the bathroom. I need a moment to compose myself and figure out what is going on.

Things have been changing since the night he randomly popped into my thoughts as a potential partner, and I don't know what to do about it. How is it that I've gotten comfortable enough with Sasha to develop an attraction to him? Of all people to develop a sexual attraction to, why does it have to be the playboy who was the most annoying person when I first met him?

# CHAPTER FIVE

RIO DARTS DOWN THE HALL, leaving me confused by his abrupt departure. Ever since the weekend that he helped me job hunt he's been acting weird, but I can't put my finger on exactly why, and I don't have time to think about it now either. Monster is still waiting for my response.

"Sadly, no," I answer his question on a sigh, pouting at the same time. "Which is a travesty, really. I would be a perfect fit there."

Monster laughs his cheeks still the brightest shade of pink. I love how easily he gets flustered, but he doesn't let that stop him either. I have no idea what it would be like to be on the ace-spectrum. I can only imagine it's confusing as fuck. Especially growing up in sports when the majority of the guys you hang out with are constantly talking about sex and girls. I mean, all that was on my mind as a teenager was sex. Of course, I wasn't thinking about girls, and that wasn't something I was able to or wanted to hide.

People tried to bully me for my flamboyancy, but I never gave a fuck. That's something I learned from my mother at a young age. She told me that there are always going to be people who don't like me, and if I let their opinions of me matter, then I'd live my entire life chasing a joy that I could never catch. If I wanted to be truly happy in this life, I had to find joy inside myself. People can say what they want about me, but the only thing that matters is what I believe.

I forgot her lesson one time, and it almost killed me.

Maybe if she wasn't taken away from me by a drunk driver when I was fifteen, I wouldn't have made that mistake. There isn't a day that goes by that I don't miss her and wish she wasn't taken from me far too soon. I can't change the past, though. I just have to keep living and try to remember all the amazing things she taught me.

"Where are you working then?" Monster asks, pulling me out of my thoughts.

"The last place you'd expect me to be working," I tell him, shaking my head, still in disbelief myself.

How did a nerd like me, who only watches sports when I'm wanting to hook up with someone, get a job as the school mascot?

Monster's brows pull together, his lips purse, and he stares at the ceiling, probably trying to figure out on his own what my new job is. Eventually he shakes his head and makes eye contact with me again. "I've got nothing."

I chuckle, patting his shoulder. "It's okay. Thinking can be hard for you athletes," I tease, and he shrugs my hand off while sticking his tongue out at me.

"The dumb jock joke is getting old," he murmurs, but there is a hint of a smirk on his lips, and I take that as the go ahead to continue teasing him from time to time.

"You know I'm just bugging you," I remind him.

His smile grows, and he nods, confirming I didn't cross a line.

"And to stop you from thinking too hard, I'll put you out of your misery and tell you what my new gig is," I tell him with a smirk. "I'm the newest member of the GSU mascot team." I throw my arms up in a *ta-da* manner, not missing the way Monster's jaw drops.

"You are the newest Kerrington?" Rio asks, causing me to jump. I didn't hear him walking back to us.

I turn to him with a plastered-on smile. "Yup," I reply, popping the p. "I know I'm new to this gig, but I'm nailing it if I do say so myself." I wink at him, noticing he has the same look of shock on his face as Monster does.

"You're right," Monster finally says. "That is the last job I would have thought you'd apply for. How did you get the position anyway? Don't they fill that at the beginning of the year with auditions and all that shit?"

I nod. "That's what I've been told, but they had a last-minute vacancy and needed to fill it immediately. So my bad luck of being forced out of a job suddenly turned out in their favor, and here we are."

"You have a lot more energy than the other mascots," Rio notes, causing me to stand a little taller at his praise.

I love being told when I'm doing a good job. Which is something I've been hearing from Evangeline a lot since I started training to be the newest Kerrington. I've spent the past three days working my ass off to learn the routines, but thankfully, they came easily to me. Tonight was my first time being on the field for a game. I'll admit I was nervous since I've barely had any training time, but Evangeline wanted to see what I was capable of in a real-life environment. It went better than I ever could have imagined. Evangeline was singing my praise, and all the cheerleaders were telling me they hope I get put on the schedule more because I was the most fun Mascot they'd worked with in a long time. I'm still trying not to let their words get to my head.

"You were at the soccer game tonight?" Monster asks, connecting the dots.

"Yup, it was my first game. How do you think I did?"

"Amazing," Rio and Monster say at the same time, and I chuckle.

"Thank you. I had a blast. I'm not going to lie, and I

wasn't sold that this job would be the best fit for me. I was afraid I would get bored on the sidelines, but that didn't happen at all. The cheerleaders welcomed me with open arms, and the crowd ate up my antics. I could easily get addicted to that kind of praise."

"You don't mind that they are cheering for Kerrington and not actually you?" Rio asks. "I thought you liked being the center of attention."

"I *love* being the center of attention," I correct him. "The fact that people don't know it's me inside the costume almost makes it more fun. And if I fuck up, I won't have to tiptoe around waiting for the awkwardness to fade because most people will have no idea it's me inside the koala."

"I see your logic there," Monster says. "I really enjoyed how over the top you were today. The crowd was definitely eating up all your moves. Do you think the other mascots will get jealous?"

I shrug. "If they do, that's on them. Not my fault they can't move like I do."

Evangeline voiced her concern when I first told her I wanted to add more flips and energy to my routine because the majority of the other team members don't have the ability to do the same, but when she saw the way the crowd reacted, she ate her words. I know it's rude to step on people's toes, but I always put my all into everything I do. The last thing I would want to do is half-ass this job just to appease the other team members. Hopefully, they don't end up hating me, but I could live with it if they do.

"I wish I had your confidence," Monster mumbles.

"Is it confidence or cockiness?" Rio questions.

"My mom taught me that people's opinions of me don't matter," I tell Monster, ignoring Rio's remark. "There are always going to be people who don't like me or think I need to be different. If you spend all your time trying to make other people happy, you'll never be truly happy yourself.

You have to live your life for yourself. Those that matter will love you for you. If you have to change yourself to make someone like you, they'll never really love you. It will always be conditional, and eventually, they'll find a reason to leave. Or they'll keep asking you to change until you don't even recognize yourself anymore."

"That makes so much sense," Monster replies, with a nod of his head.

"If you want lessons on being awesome, let me know," I tell him, earning me a laugh in response. "But in the meantime, let's make some popcorn and get this movie marathon started."

"Fuck yeah," Monster cheers, heading toward the kitchen.

I'm about to follow him, but Rio grabs my elbow, stopping me. Jolts of electricity shoot up my arm from his touch, and I have to fight myself from sucking in a breath of air. He doesn't need to know that I react like this to him.

"I know we aren't exactly close friends, but if you ever want to talk, I'm here for you," he tells me with a soft smile.

There he goes, acting nice again. What the hell has come over this guy?

I've never talked about my past with anyone, except a therapist before, wanting to forget about it, but Rio's offer has me wondering if I should change that. Maybe I should open up to someone about the horrible things I went through, but should that person be Rio?

"Thanks," I whisper and nibble on my lower lip.

He opens his mouth to say something else, but the door opens before he can get the words out. His hand drops from my elbow as his roommate enters, and I miss his touch already, which is stupid since he only meant it in a friendly manner.

"Sorry I'm late," Bronny apologizes as he enters the apartment.

I'm dying to know what Rio was about to say, but the moment is over,

"You're right on time," I correct Bronny. "Monster is making the popcorn now."

"Perfect," he replies with a wide, toothy grin. "I'll change super quick."

He leaves me and Rio alone again and I struggle to find words. Which is not something that happens to me often. I find myself staring into his eyes. He doesn't look away, and a warmth I hadn't expected tingles up my spine.

Monster grumbles something from the other room, breaking the moment.

"We should go make sure Monster doesn't burn the popcorn," Rio says, and I nod, still struggling to form a sentence. So, instead of talking, I head to the kitchen with Rio right behind me.

Something is definitely going on with that man and I wonder if I should say something. The fact that he has offered to be a listening ear if I need one is a huge step for us. Maybe that means I can finally get him to say yes to a date with me. Not that I've actually asked him out before, more like just offered up a night of fun, but I think I'd be willing to date again for him.

# CHAPTER SIX

MY BRAIN IS a bit of a mess as I make my way to the athletics facility on Monday morning. I had the weirdest dreams all weekend long, and I have no idea what they could mean.

"Ready for coach to kick our asses today at training?" BooBoo asks when I enter the locker room.

"You know it," I reply with a wink. "There isn't anything coach can throw at me that I can't handle."

BooBoo grins from ear to ear and pats me on the shoulder. "That's my man."

I grab my gear from my locker but before I change I notice BooBoo playing with the pendant he always wears and a random thought pops into my head causing me to pause. "It was you that was talking about your mom being into witchy stuff, wasn't it?"

"Yup, made for a lot of weird shit going on in the house growing up," he replies. "I still don't understand most of it, but it makes Mom happy, and she isn't hurting anyone so I go along with it."

It doesn't surprise me that BooBoo lets his mom have her way even if he doesn't understand things because that's just the kind of guy he is. He wants everyone around him to be happy. He's the type to go along with just about anything to bring a smile to the faces of the people he cares about.

"Why the sudden questions about my witchy mom? You thinking about trying that stuff out?"

I shake my head. "No. I was just wondering if you knew anything about what certain dreams mean."

He tilts his head to the side. "What have you been dreaming about?"

I cast a quick glance around the room to make sure no one is listening to our conversation before leaning closer to BooBoo. "I keep dreaming that I'm being chased by a Koala," I whisper.

"Interesting," he responds in a softened tone, staring intently at me.

"Do you know what that means?" I ask, holding my breath as I wait for his response.

"Not a fucking clue," he tells me with a smirk. I roll my eyes giving his shoulder a shove for getting me going like that. He laughs and holds his hands up. "But I'm pretty sure my mom has a book about what dreams mean. I should be able to run over there tonight and grab it if you want. We can read it on the bus ride tomorrow."

"Why not," I reply. "If I can figure out *why* I'm having these odd dreams, maybe then I'll stop having them."

BooBoo purses his lips and nods. "Who knew having a mother like mine would pay off."

I chuckle with him, then change into my clothes for training. When I'm done, I chat with BooBoo about his weekend. Eventually, Whiley joins us, complaining that his sink burst a pipe this morning, and he was afraid he wasn't going to be able to make it on time for practice. Thankfully, that didn't happen because the coach isn't too pleased when guys are late.

Just as Whiley finishes changing, coach enters the locker room for our pre-training meeting.

The meeting runs as expected, going over what we need to work on and a breakdown of the strengths and weaknesses of the team we'll be playing tomorrow. But when I think he's about to dismiss us, he brings up something new.

"I know we don't normally have our mascot with us on away games," Coach starts. "But since our newest Kerrington is still in training, Evangeline has requested he join us for our game tomorrow. I figured having the presence of our friendly and energetic Koala could only bring us good luck, so I agreed. I expect you all to treat Sasha with respect and give him a warm welcome. He might not be a member of this soccer team, but he is a part of the GSU athletics family and deserves to be treated like you would treat anyone else on this team. Do I make myself clear?"

"Yes, Sir," we all shout at the same time.

"Excellent, now let's get to the pitch," he says before heading out of the locker room.

To say I'm unprepared to find out that Sasha will be traveling with us tomorrow is an understatement. I knew I would be seeing a lot more of him now that he's our newest mascot, but I thought away games were a safe space to avoid these new feelings that Sasha has brought up. Apparently, I was wrong.

I don't think it would have bothered me if this news had been sprung on me a week ago, I've always been good at ignoring him when he gets too annoying. But after this weekend and finding out that I might be attracted to him, the last thing I want is to spend a two-hour bus ride with him sitting right beside me. I spent far too much of my time thinking about him over the weekend, and I was hoping to get some time away from him in the place where I'm always able to push away my thoughts and clear my mind.

Fingers crossed he finds someone else to sit with.

SLEEP WAS FILLED with more bizarre dreams of being chased by a Koala, leaving me more confused and wanting to get my hands on that book BooBoo told me about.

As I eat my breakfast and get my gear ready for the trip I'm moving at a snail's pace and my brain is a foggy mess. I hate feeling like this.

My feet are dragging as I make my way to the bus, and I just pray I can clear out the cobwebs before we have to play. I don't want to be a liability to our team.

As usual, I'm one of the first guys to arrive at the bus, so I throw my gear bag underneath and lean against the side until more of my teammates arrive.

To my utter shock, Sasha shows up only moments after me. I've never known him to be on time for anything.

"Why do you look like a dear caught in headlights?" he asks me as he adjusts his backpack on his shoulders.

"I think this is the first time I've ever witnessed you not late for an event," I supply, making Sasha laugh loudly.

"Well, considering I get paid for this, I didn't want to make a bad impression," he tells me while brushing a lock of his long blonde hair out of his face.

"Good idea. Although you are charming enough that even if you were late, I'm sure you could talk your way out of getting into any trouble."

"You think I'm charming?" he inquires with a flirtatious smile.

I roll my eyes like I always do, but I contemplate telling him the truth that not only do I find him charming, but that I'm attracted to him too.

Before I'm able to come up with a plan, Evangeline arrives, and Sasha excuses himself to talk to her, leaving me alone and a bit relieved. I don't think I'm ready to tell him about my feelings toward him just yet. If I'm being honest with myself, I don't even know what my feelings are for

Sasha. I should probably get that figured out before I start confessing things.

Thankfully it doesn't take long for BooBoo to arrive, and he heads directly over to me.

"Did you get the book?" I question, anxious to find out the answers I hope it holds.

"I did, and you totally owe me one," he grumbles while riffling through his backpack. "I had to spend three hours talking to my mom about witchy stuff. I'm pretty sure my brain is never going to be the same after that conversation." He stops talking and hands me a clear-ish stone.

I tilt my head to the side, pursing my lips. "Umm, thanks?" I blink at my friend a couple of times, wondering why he just gave me a rock.

BooBoo sighs before responding. "Mom made me promise I would give that to you. It's supposed to help with clarity. It's a clear quartz, you're supposed to keep it on you at all times, even sleep with it under your pillow."

"Oookaayy…" I draw out.

"Did you want me to tell her no?" he asks with a raised brow.

I shake my head. "No, but why would she think I need clarity?"

"In order to borrow the book, I had to tell her about your dream," he explains. "I hope that isn't like an invasion of your privacy or something," he adds on quickly.

I wave him off. I've only briefly met his mom at a couple of games, but she seemed like a nice lady, and I'm not very concerned about her knowing about my dreams. "It's all good. Did she have any insight into what it could mean?"

BooBoo pulls the book out, opening it to a page that is bookmarked with a Kleenex. "According to the book and Mom, dreams about being chased tend to mean you are afraid of or are trying to avoid something. Hence, the quartz. Mom says once your mind is clear, you'll know exactly what the dream means."

I scrap my scalp and sigh. "Does the Koala mean anything?"

BooBoo nods, pulling out another book. "Mom says typically in running dreams, you're trying to get away from the subject you are afraid of, but we both know you don't have a fear of koalas, so she gave me this book about dream animals." Another Kleenex hangs out of the top of this book, and he opens it to the marked page. "Apparently, koala dreams can have a bunch of different meanings, but the one that goes the most with your running dream is that your subconscious mind is trying to tell you to let things unfold at their own pace."

I don't respond immediately, trying to wrap my head around all he just told me, flipping the quartz around in my hand a couple of times. "Does any of this make sense to you?" I ask my friend after a few moments pass.

He scoffs. "It all sounds like crazy shit to me," he tells me. "But what *I* think doesn't matter. It only matters if this resonates with *you* or not."

I nod, unsure if what the books are telling me truly hits home or not.

"Mom also said she'd be happy to do a tarot reading for you if you'd be interested."

"Have you had one done before?" I check with a tilt of my head.

He laughs at my question like I'm crazy for even asking. "Only like a million. I'll admit, as much as I think my mom is looney sometimes, her readings have always been scarily accurate. They are also really open to interpretation, though, and sometimes you'll think the cards mean one thing when they actually mean something else."

I stare at the quartz in my hand and nibble on my lower

lip. "I'll think about it. Mind if I keep the books for the day," I ask. "I'd like to read the passages all the way through."

"Totally. Keep them as long as you need them," he assures me with an even smile.

"Thanks," I reply, shoving the books into my backpack and the quartz into my pocket.

The stone sits heavy in the small space, never letting me forget about its presence. Is it going to help me figure out my dreams? I've never been a person who believes in this kind of stuff, but the dreams have been happening for four nights now and there is this nudging sensation deep in my gut that is telling me it means something. So, if this stupid rock will give me the answers, I'm all for it.

# CHAPTER SEVEN

Sasha

THERE'S a giant smile on my face as I talk with Evangeline about everything I'm to expect on this adventure. Okay, it's *technically* not an adventure, but it feels like one to me. I've never been more excited to be trapped on a bus with a bunch of sweaty soccer players in my life. Wait, why does that sound like the makings of a porno? I give my head a shake at the completely random thought and continue my journey to the waiting team and my boss.

"Are you excited for your first away game?" Evangeline asks me, and I nod exuberantly.

"Beyond excited," I correct her. "I can't wait to put on a show even if I'll only be on the sidelines."

Apparently, when you're the mascot for the opposing team you don't get to be front and center like you do at home games. Which I'll admit is totally lame, but I'll still give my all from the small amount of space I'll be allotted.

"Even from the sidelines, you're going to kill it," Rebecca, one of the cheerleaders who will be by my side tonight, tells me with a wide grin.

"One hundred percent. You're a star and will shine wherever you are," Hailey, the other cheerleader coming on this trip, adds.

I smile brightly at both the girls, then flick my hand at them in an '*oh you*' kind of motion. "Stop buttering me up like that, or my head will get too big to fit in the costume," I tease, earning a giggle from both of them.

"Oh, you love hearing how amazing you are," Hailey says, knowing me so well already.

I shrug. No point in denying it.

"Come on, let's go get our seats before the guys take all the good ones," Rebecca urges us, but I motion for them to go on.

"I'll be right there, but I'm going to talk to a friend first," I tell them as they make their way onto the bus. I walk toward Rio, who is chatting with a few of his teammates. Are you guys ready to win?" I ask them when I arrive.

"Always," one of the guys with shaggy dark brown hair and a killer smile says to me.

I narrow my brows at him and stare for a moment until he starts to squirm.

"Why is he looking at me like that?" the guy whispers to Rio.

"Because he's crazy," Rio replies with a shrug.

"I'm just trying to figure out if you're being cocky or confident," I tell the guy.

"Does it matter?" he questions with a pinched expression.

I scoff and roll my eyes. "Obviously. Confidence is attractive and admirable. Cockiness makes you a douche. Soooo…" I draw out the word. "Are you saying you're ready because you've trained your ass off and know you can handle whatever is thrown at you? Oooorrr, are you saying it because you think it makes you look tough?"

Rio presses his lips together, his eyes shining with the laughter he's holding back, but the other man standing with them can't control himself and lets out a bark of a laugh.

The brunette flips off his friend, then rolls his shoulders back and meets my gaze. "I'm confident," he replies with a straight spine and firm tip of his chin.

"Good," I reply with a smirk and stick my hand out. "I'm Sasha, by the way, the newest Kerrington."

"I'm Rob, but everyone calls me BooBoo," he replies, shaking my hand.

"I'm Whiley," the other man with dirty blonde hair and stunning green eyes tells me, taking my hand after BooBoo lets go.

"Is that your real name?" I check, even though I'm almost certain it's not.

He shakes his head with a toothy smile. "Nope, but I don't give that out to anyone."

"*We* don't even know his real first name," Rio supplies.

"And I think the only reason we know his last name is because it's printed on his jersey," BooBoo adds.

Whiley lifts a shoulder. "Maybe I just like to be mysterious."

"Rumor on the street is he's a serial killer and kills anyone who finds out his real name," BooBoo stage whispers, making Whiley roll his eyes, but he doesn't deny said rumor either… interesting.

"Time to get on the bus," the coach calls out in a booming voice.

All of us head toward the door at the same time, not wanting to be on Coach's bad side. Whiley and BooBoo are ahead, and Rio is right behind me.

"Do you have a seat partner yet?" I ask him as we get on.

"I always sit with BooBoo," he answers. "You could probably sit with Whiley if you want."

"And risk being murdered?" I whisper in mock horror.

Rio chuckles. "I don't think he's *actually* a serial killer."

"Well, I'd rather be safe than sorry," I respond, scanning the seats and noticing Evangeline has an empty spot next to her, across the aisle from the cheerleaders. "Oh, look, a free seat next to not a serial killer," I state, pointing toward Evangeline, who smiles and waves at me.

"How do you know she isn't a serial killer?" Rio whispers into my ear in a deep, breathy tone.

The hairs on the back of my neck stand up, and goosebumps cover my arms. Not from the words, which are innocent, but from my stupid imagination that is now conjuring up different scenarios of him whispering in my ear. Thoughts that have no place running around in my brain at this moment. I fight back the lustful shiver that wants to escape as my mind travels straight into the gutter.

I flash a smile at him over my shoulder, hoping he doesn't realize that his voice turned me on. "I'll take my chances with the one who *doesn't* have the rumor about her," I tell him, then take the seat next to my boss.

"See you later," he responds as he passes me to sit with his friends.

"Making new friends?" Evangeline asks with a warm grin.

"Kind of. BooBoo and Whiley are new, but I've known Rio a while now," I supply.

"That's excellent. It's always good to be on happy terms with the team," she responds. "The last thing we want is animosity between our mascot and the players."

"Has that happened before?" I check, earning me a sigh.

"Unfortunately, it's happened more than I would like to admit. And it's always over the dumbest things."

"I promise not to make any waves," I assure her. "Besides, everyone always loves me." I wink at her, and she shoves my shoulder in a playful way.

"Didn't I overhear you tell BooBoo not to be cocky?" she questions with a knowing smile and a lifted brow.

"I'm not being cocky. I'm *confident* that everyone loves me," I reply, making her laugh.

It doesn't take long for the rest of the team to board the bus and we are finally on our way to my first away game as Kerrington the Koala.

# CHAPTER EIGHT

## Rio

THE BOOKS BOOBOO lent me are in my lap, one on top of the other. I keep reading the words on the page over and over again. Maybe if I focus hard enough, I'll be able to interpret the dream.

What am I possibly afraid of or trying to avoid?

I fish out the quartz from my pocket, flipping it around in my hand a few times as I try to figure out the answer.

A chorus of laughter from the front of the bus pulls my attention from the words that I've almost memorized already.

As I lean my head into the aisle, I see Sasha telling a story in his vibrant personality filled way. His hands are flying around as he speaks, and the people around him are doubled over as they listen to whatever the man has to say.

"That Sasha guy seems like a good time," BooBoo notes as he lifts himself to peek over the seat in front of him to see what everyone is cackling about.

"He loves being the center of attention, that's for sure," I respond, then return my focus to the book.

"How long have you known him?" my friend asks, and I blow out a breath through my nose before giving him my attention again.

Maybe a small break from my reading will be good anyway. It's not like I've had any epiphanies in the last forty-five minutes of studying the words.

"I met Sasha like two years ago when Chase started dating Gabriel who is one of Sasha's best friends," I tell him. "He kind of just stuck around even after Chase left. Sasha is one of those guys that as soon as you let him in, he never leaves."

BooBoo chuckles while shaking his head. "He doesn't seem like a bad guy, so it could be worse," he states. I still can't believe you're best friends with Chase Anderson," he adds like he does every time I bring up Chase.

"He's just a regular guy," I remind him for probably the hundredth time.

"He is *not* a regular guy," BooBoo retorts. "He's a legend in the making. He's already breaking NFL records, and he's only just starting his second year with the Michigan Raptors."

I shrug. I get why he's a little starstruck. Chase *is* incredibly talented. But he's also a genuine guy, and sometimes it's easy to forget that he's an NFL superstar now.

Another roar of laughter flutters down from the front of the bus, and suddenly, I wish I was sitting closer to Sasha to hear what he's talking about.

"Hopefully, he brings that personality to the game tonight. Maybe he'll even get the opposing fans cheering for us," BooBoo says, nudging his elbow into my arm.

I chuckle and shake my head. Honestly, I could see Sasha doing just that. As annoying as he was when I first met him, he has a way of worming into your heart and staying there like a parasite. At first, I wanted to do everything in my power to get him away from me, but I learned very quickly that you don't just get rid of Sasha. At least, that was my experience. Not that I'll tell him that.

THERE ARE a lot of GSU fans in the stands tonight. My

eyes sweep to the crowd as we make our way onto the pitch, and I notice half of them are dressed in green.

Sasha, dressed in the Kerrington costume, lifts his arms, and the cheerleaders on either side of him shake their pompoms as they get the crowd going. The fans yell and cheer us on, and it brings a huge smile to my face.

Away games can be a bit nerve wracking when the majority of the people in the stands are hoping that you lose, but tonight, it's a good fifty-fifty split, which helps to ease the stress.

"Let's kick some ass," BooBoo shouts as we get into position.

My focus narrows to the here and now, tuning out the fans and everything outside of the pitch. All that matters at this moment are my teammates, the opposing players, and, most importantly, the ball.

I take a deep inhale of the cool air as I wait for the ball to get in motion. My heart beats steadily in my chest and a confident grin spreads across my face as I stare down the team we're playing.

# CHAPTER NINE

THE GAME IS A NAILBITER, and I find myself watching Rio like a fucking hawk as he runs across the turf of the field, or should I say *pitch*. Don't want to forget that and have the coach correct me again with the most boring spiel. Does it really matter what I call it?

Internally, I give my head a shake, returning my focus to the game that is currently tied four-four. Every time our team scores, the other team does the exact same, keeping us at a tie and on our toes. I'm dying to find out who's going to win.

Rio has been killing it the entire game. I've been sneaking glances at him any chance I get, which turns out to be a lot. He has the ball now and is racing toward the net. I wish I could run as fast as these guys, or maybe I don't... running isn't very fun. But being fast is. Rio's gaze is glued to the net as he gets closer and pulls back one of his powerful legs then snaps it forward, sending the ball flying directly into the net.

The half of the crowd that is cheering for our team loses their shit, and Rebecca and Hailey shake their pompoms as our guys shout and hug each other. When Rebecca elbows me, I realize I'm standing there staring instead of jumping up and down like I'm supposed to be doing. With a quick inhale, I throw my hands up and turn my head from side to side to make sure I have enough space to do a backflip.

"Stand clear," I say to the girls since there is no way the crowd could hear me.

Hailey and Rebecca step to the side, and I do a cartwheel followed by a perfect back flip, which has our fans shouting even louder—which is surprising since they were already pretty loud.

I jump up and down, and the girls flank my sides again as we hype the crowd up some more before the game gets back in motion.

"How are you doing?" Evangeline asks once the ball is moving again, and I'm able to sit for a moment on the bench.

"Hot," I reply, then take a sip of the water in my hydration pack on my back, which has a tube sticking out by my neck.

She smiles at me and nods. "It takes getting used to I hear."

"At least I won't be packing any water weight," I joke, and she giggles.

"You'll be in the best shape of your life by the end of the school year."

I nod, then stand and tilt my head toward Hailey and Rebecca, who join me. I start shouting out a simple cheer for the crowd to join in on to help encourage our guys to get another goal.

I follow the movements of the girls, stepping from side to side and clapping my hands to the beat of the cheer.

After a few minutes we take another break and watch the game that is still just as intense as it has been all evening.

Our team has possession of the ball, and Rio passes to Whiley with perfect precision. Whiley kicks the ball—I mean dribbles it down the pitch—before passing to BooBoo, who gives the ball back to Rio. The plays go so quickly that it's almost hard to follow, but thankfully, this time, our team is able to keep ahold of the ball, and for the third time tonight, Rio scores for our team.

This time, I don't freeze, and I immediately break out into

a couple of cartwheels to celebrate the goal. We are finally two points ahead of the opponents, and the game is almost over. A giddy energy races through my veins, and I can almost taste the victory. I know it's best not to get too excited because anything can happen, but I'm holding onto the positive thinking that we are going to win.

"Give me a G," Hailey shouts during a brief pause in the game, then points her pompom to the crowd, who repeat the letter back to her.

"Give me a S," Rebecca calls out next, and the fans respond even louder this time.

"Give me a U," Hailey takes the lead again, this time holding her pompom to her ear as she waits for the thunderous reply.

"What's that spell?" the girls yell at the same time.

"GSU," the crowd shouts back.

"What's that spell?"

"GSU."

"What's that spell?"

"GSU!" The crowd is so loud at this point I almost fall over from their contagious energy.

"Let's go GSU!" the girls call out a couple of times, and the crowd joins in, cheering our boys on with so much enthusiasm it's mind boggling.

The guys who are sitting on the sideline are grinning from ear to ear from the support the crowd is showing them, and the players on the field look even more determined than they were.

There is no doubt in my mind that we are going to win the game tonight.

When the clock hits ten seconds to go, the crowd starts to count down—something I found out last game is a tradition in college soccer—and when the buzzer rings out, our side of the stands loses its mind with cheers, hollers, and cries of pure joy.

The players who were on the sideline race on to the pitch to celebrate with the rest of the team and I'm left in aww of how amazing it feels to be experiencing this moment with the team right now.

"Get out there," Evangeline encourages me, and I quickly listen, cartwheeling and front-handspringing my way to the team.

I high-five the players when I reach them and throw up a few of their arms, waving them toward the crowd, who are all on their feet, still cheering.

"We did it, boys!" BooBoo screams.

Pure adrenaline races through my veins as I celebrate the win with the team. I can only imagine how the players feel at this moment, to have accomplished what they set out to do tonight. I know this is just one game of many more to come, but a win is a win in my books. As the team continues to cheer and show their joy, my gaze lands on Rio, who's smiling so big it damn near takes up his whole face. His jersey is clinging to his body from how sweaty he is, and his light brown hair is a mess, but he's still hot as fuck.

Fuck. What I wouldn't do for a chance to form a deeper connection with him.

Eventually, the coaching team escorts us off the field, and I find Evangeline waiting for me in the change area that was set up for me and the cheerleaders while the guys change in a different locker room.

"You killed it tonight," Evangeline tells me as she helps me take off the koala head.

I beam at her when I'm free and grab a towel to wipe the sweat off my forehead.

"I don't think I've had this much fun at a job in a long time," I tell her as she helps me out of the costume. "And I really loved teaching dance."

"I really hope you don't ever lose that joy for this position," she says, then hands me a bottle of water.

I gulp down the blissful coldness, relishing in how good it feels sliding down my throat.

"I'll admit there are downsides to this job," I tell my boss, who frowns a little until I finish my thought. "But the positives far outweigh the negatives. The energy of the crowd the past few games has been intoxicating."

"Wait until we lose a game," Hailey mumbles over her shoulder as she changes out of her skimpy cheerleading outfit.

"It's like the exact opposite feeling in the stadium," Rebecca adds.

"How likely is it that I won't ever have to experience that?" I check before dashing behind a curtain to change out of my sweaty clothes.

"An undefeated season is the dream of every college athletics team, but it's one very few have ever done," Evangeline tells me. "And since you'll be cheering for multiple teams, not just this soccer team, it's even *more* likely that you'll witness at least one loss."

I nod as I come out of the changing area and stuff my gross clothes into my bag. "I guess that makes sense," I murmur, already hating the idea of a loss.

"Losing sucks, but it makes the next win even better," Rebecca states, which helps turn the corners of my lips upward.

"As long as I have you two beauties by my side, it won't matter if we win or lose."

Hailey giggles and then throws a towel at me. "How is a man so sweet as you still single?"

"You think a wild stallion like me is easy to break?" I question with a raised brow. "I like having fun, and I'm not looking to settle down anytime soon."

What I don't admit is actually wanting to date one guy in particular, but I'm pretty sure he isn't into me at all.

"Oh, it's going to be so fun watching you fall in love," she replies.

I roll my eyes in response. "Love is for the weak."

"You're just tempting the love gods to hit you with their arrows," Rebecca voices.

"Yup, those that protest too much about love are always the ones that fall the hardest," Hailey adds.

"I've done love once; I won't be doing it again," I tell them. "But if you know any single queer guys who are up for a night of fun, send them my way." I wink, then grab my backpack, throwing it over my shoulder. "Are we ready to go, or do I have to sit here and listen to you gossip about my love life some more?"

"We're ready," Hailey says. "But don't think we won't continue this conversation on the bus." The smile that she offers me when she walks by is sweet and deadly at the same time.

Note to self: do not get on that girl's bad side.

# CHAPTER TEN

## *TEN DAYS LATER*

THE BUS IS ALMOST silent tonight. It is filled with frowns and broken hearts as we make the drive back to the GSU campus. We lost our away game last night so badly it was fucking pathetic. Coach reamed us out after the game, and we deserved it. We hadn't lost a single game this season until last night, and it stings.

"I know last night was a tough loss, but I don't want it to keep you down forever," Coach tells us as we pull into the campus parking lot. "We have another game on Tuesday, and I know you can pull it around."

We all nod our heads and quietly respond, " Yes, Coach," before getting off the bus.

"I wish I knew why we sucked so bad last night," BooBoo grumbles as we grab our bags.

Me too, man, but there's nothing we can do about it. We just have to pick ourselves up and try to do better at our next game."

He nods, then heads toward his parked car, and I do the same.

As I make my way to my apartment all I can think about is having a nap. I barely got any sleep last night, and the small amount I managed wasn't restful at all. At least the upside of a shit sleep was the fact that I didn't have any weird dreams.

The elevator slowly takes me to my floor, and my feet shuffle against the carpet as I head to my apartment. My thoughts are solely on getting sleep, so I'm completely caught off guard when I'm greeted with a giant bear hug that almost steals the air from my lungs. Fuck, Sasha's a lot stronger than he looks.

"I'm so sorry about your loss," he coos into my ear while holding me tightly.

"What are you doing here?" I grumble as he continues to hug me. Part of me thinks I should be pushing him away, but the embrace actually feels nice. I've never allowed Sasha to comfort me like this before, but I don't hate it, even though I probably should. I actually kind of like it.

"I didn't think you should be alone after a loss like that," he says, finally loosening his embrace, but his hands don't leave my body, which, again, I don't hate. His touch is comforting and is helping to ease some of the disappointment I've been harboring since the loss of the game. "Monster told me he was busy with his sister today, and Bronny had plans with some other friends. Both of them offered to cancel their previous arrangements, but I told them I would be here for you."

"I just want to nap," I respond, trying to step to the side.

"That's fine. I'll be here when you're ready," he tells me, finally stepping back and letting me fully enter my apartment.

When he removes his hands from my arms, I miss his touch, which leaves me confused. Although that seems to be a common emotion around Sasha these days, I should probably try to decipher my feelings more, but I'm far too exhausted to do that right now.

"You don't have to do that," I assure him, dropping my

bag by the door. Normally, I'm not a slob, but I don't have the energy to care about the mess at the moment.

"I know I don't have to, but I want to. You offered to be a listening ear for me the other day. I'm doing the same now. Even if you don't want to talk, I'm not going anywhere. I'll sit here in silence and study, but I'm not leaving you so you can wallow in self-hate."

I sigh. "How do you know I'm going to wallow?"

Sasha rolls his eyes dramatically and scoffs. "We might not be best friends, but I know you well enough to know you sulk after a loss, and I'm not going to stand for it today."

"There's nothing I can say to get you to leave, is there?" I check.

He shakes his head with a toothy grin. "Now go take your nap if you must. I'll be here when you're ready for some company," he tells me before heading to the living room and plopping himself onto one of the recliners.

I shake my head, making my way to my room, but notice there is a hint of a smile on my lips at the idea of Sasha not leaving. I've always wanted to be left alone after losses, but knowing there is someone here for me, whether I like it or not, is kind of comforting.

Sasha is right that we've never been best friends, and his pushiness has often been beyond annoying to me, but this time, I don't hate it. Maybe it's because my feelings for him have been evolving over the past couple of weeks, and I can't seem to get him out of my head, no matter how hard I try.

I close the door behind me and undress, placing the quartz from my pocket under my pillow like I've done every night since BooBoo gave it to me. I don't feel like it's offered me any sort of clarity, but I can't find it in me to stop carrying it around with me. Everywhere I go, that stupid stone goes.

With how exhausted I am the moment my head hits my pillow I'm pulled into a deep sleep, but of course am met with the stupid dream that won't leave me alone. Maybe it's time to see BooBoo's mom and get that tarot reading. I can't continue to live with my dreams being haunted by something that makes zero sense to me.

IT'S early evening by the time I finally wake. My stomach grumbles at me, offended that it hasn't been fed in far too long. I should have set an alarm so I didn't nap so late since it will be almost impossible to sleep tonight, but I was exhausted and needed the rest.

I throw on a pair of sweats and a GSU hoodie before deciding to go on the hunt for food, but come up short when I open my door and am met by my duffle bag resting on the floor. I furrow my brows. How in the world did it get here? My brain is still filled with sleep, and for the life of me, I can't come up with an answer, so I shrug and drag it into my room. What throws me for another loop is the fact that the zipper is open, so I quickly dig through my things wondering who the hell opened my bag.

A tiny gasp slips past my lips when I realize *why* my bag is open. Someone washed all of my gear and folded the items neatly before putting them back in. Who the hell would do something like that?

I give my head a shake then make my way down the hall to where Sasha, Monster, and Bronny are playing video games.

"Who did my laundry?" I question, leaning against the wall.

"I did," Sasha tells me with a wide smile. "And don't worry, I called BooBoo first to make sure I didn't wreck anything."

I'm taken aback by his words. That feels like a lot of effort to go through for someone who he even admitted isn't his best friend.

"Thank you," I whisper, unsure what else to say.

"I also made you some food," he says while turning his focus back to the game. "The plate is in the fridge; all you have to do is warm it up."

I stare at him like he's grown a second head. I know he told me he was going to be here for me today, but I'm still shocked and a bit in awe that he did so much for me, all because I had a bad day. I've seen Sasha's sweet side a few times over the years I've known him, but it's never been directed toward me like this, and I don't know how to process it.

Instead of saying anything, I just dip my chin and head to the kitchen to see what he made. My hopes aren't high, considering Sasha always burns the popcorn on movie nights and one time he almost set the apartment on fire when him and Monster tried to make some sort of deep-fried dish.

My jaw damn near hits the floor when my eyes land on a plate of chicken, rice, and veggies waiting for me. I know I slept for several hours but this man not only did my laundry, but he cooked a meal for me that is exactly what I would have made for myself. BooBoo probably filled Sasha in on my meal plan while he was telling him how to do my laundry.

I don't think I've ever had someone take care of me like this before, and I don't know how to react.

"I hope I cooked everything okay," Sasha says, joining me in the kitchen as I place the plate in the microwave. "I followed the recipe BooBoo sent me, and I cut the chicken to make sure it wasn't pink inside, but cooking isn't always my strong suit."

"Why did you do all of this?" I ask while staring at the microwave.

"It's what friends do," he tells me, and I can see him shrug his shoulders out of the corner of my eye. "You had a shitty day, and I wanted to cheer you up. You aren't one who likes it when people make a big deal about things for you, so I figured I'd just lighten your load."

Before I realize what I'm doing, I'm turning and pulling Sasha in for a hug, causing the vibrant man to squeak and stiffen before softening into my embrace and wrapping his arms around me in return.

"Thank you," I whisper as I hold him for a moment.

"You don't have to thank me. I promise it was no big deal," he responds while rubbing my back gently.

This hug feels good. His arms making me feel wanted and cared for,

I should probably let him go. The hug is going on far longer than is normal for a thank-you, but for some reason, I don't want to release him. I want to keep him in my arms. The thought alone is alarming enough to cause me to step back.

"I know you say it's no big deal, but it is to me. I really appreciate it," I tell him, and his cheeks pinken a bit. Bashful isn't a look that Sasha gets often but it's cute on him.

"Well, now that I know doing small acts of kindness can earn me a hug from the grumpy Rio, I might do them more often," he teases.

I roll my eyes, but there is a smile on my lips all the same.

The microwave beeps, and I pull my plate of food out, tilting my head. "Come on, I can eat this in the living room. I'm curious to see who's winning."

Sasha follows behind me, and I wonder what it would be like to hang out with him one-on-one. Suddenly, I want to know more about Sasha and what makes him the person he is. He has so many sides to him, and I'd like to see them all.

# CHAPTER ELEVEN

BRONNY KICKS at the coffee table and throws his controller onto the couch beside him. "Why do I fucking suck tonight?" he grumbles, then stands and stretches his arms above his head.

"You suck most of the time, but tonight is worse than usual," Monster teases.

Bronny flips him off. "Whatever. I'm done losing, so I'm going to bed," he grumbles, waving at us before disappearing down the hall.

Monster looks at his phone, and his brows shoot up. "Shit, I didn't realize it was so late I'm going to hit the hay too," he says before leaving too.

"I should not have napped as late as I did," Rio mutters. "You can head out if you want."

"I'm cool with chilling for a little longer. I haven't been sleeping the best the past couple of nights anyway," I tell him, and he nods like he understands exactly what I'm going through.

"Okay. Would you like to keep gaming or watch a movie?" he asks, and I shrug.

"Whatever you want. Today was supposed to be about making you happy, so you choose."

"Well, I'd really hate to make you cry by kicking your ass at *Mario Kart*. We should probably just watch a movie," he says, standing up to grab the controllers that his roommates left behind before they went to bed.

"How noble of you," I joke while getting more comfortable on the couch.

"Anything in particular you want to watch?" he inquires once he's put the controllers away and grabbed the television remote.

I shake my head. "As long as it's not gory, I'm fine."

"I thought you liked scary movies," he states while sitting beside me.

"I do, but there's a difference between scary and gory. I want to jump and scream and lose my shit, but I don't want to see people's guts and blood everywhere."

Rio nods while scrolling through one of the streaming services he has. "I'm not in the mood for a scary movie anyway. How about a comedy," he suggests.

"Can we watch a romcom?" I ask. "That new one about a couple who fake date each other is supposed to be hilarious."

"Sure, I haven't seen it yet," he says, then searches for the title.

"Shit," I mumble when I realize it's only available for rent. "You can pick something else. I don't want you to have to rent it just to make me happy."

Rio doesn't listen, though, and sets the movie to play. "The small rental fee isn't going to set me back," he assures me, placing his arm on the back of the couch as he gets comfortable. "And besides, I wanted to see it too."

I nibble on my lower lip, accepting that it's too late to fight about it now.

As the movie plays, both Rio and I laugh our asses off and make fun of the unrealistic shit that happens because it's a movie, and it wouldn't be as entertaining if it was too much like real life. As we watch the romcom, we both get more comfortable, and the anxiousness that was growing inside of me seems to dissolve.

"You're the king of dating. Is that a common occurrence?" Rio teases as one of the main characters goes on a horrible blind date.

I chuckle and shrug. "I'm the king of one-night stands. I don't know much about actual dates."

"It's been forever since I've been on a real date I've honestly forgotten what they're like," Rio tells me and its then I realize just how close we've gotten. Rio's side is almost flush against my arm and it causes my heart to race a little.

"I might not be the king of dating, but I bet I could knock your socks off if we ever went out," I flirt with a wink.

I expect Rio to roll his eyes at my lame joke, but instead, he stares intently at me.

"Somehow, I don't doubt that," he responds, catching me off guard.

Thankfully another laugh out loud moment happens in the movie drawing our attention to it and causing us to forget the moment.

By the time the movie is over, my sides hurt from laughing so much, and I'm wiping tears away from my eyes. I knew it was going to be good, but I was not expecting it to be this good. Maybe it's who I'm watching it with, though, that made it that much better.

"What's next?" I ask as the credits roll.

"You're not tired?" Rio checks.

"Not really," I lie.

I'm exhausted, but I can tell Rio is wide awake. It isn't fair that he has to be alone because he napped a little too long. Besides, it's not a hardship to spend time with a guy I've been crushing on for the longest time.

"Mind if we watch a war movie this time? There's this new one I've been curious about, but I think it might be a little boring if you don't like history stuff."

I wave him off. "I'm fine with whatever. Put it on."

He nods and starts the movie that I've never heard of.

It doesn't take long for my eyelids to become heavy, and it starts to get hard to keep them open. I promised Rio I'd be a good friend and stay up with him, but staying true to my word is becoming harder and harder. Eventually all the fighting in the world isn't enough to keep myself awake and slumber slowly pulls me under.

SOFT SNORING FILLS THE ROOM, pulling me from my peaceful sleep. Slowly, I blink my eyes open, trying to figure out where the snoring is coming from.

Where am I, and what time is it?

As my eyes adjust to the bright room, I realize I'm on the couch at Rio, Monster, and Bronny's place, but the pillow I'm resting my head on isn't exactly a pillow. I mean, as far as I know, pillows don't have the ability to move on their own, and this one is gently twitching beneath my head. Glancing down, I see that the *"pillow"* is, in fact, someone's knees.

It's then I remember watching movies with Rio and falling asleep during the second one. I guess I must have gotten comfortable in his lap at some point. By the sound of his even breathing and adorable snoring, Rio fell asleep at some point too, but only he knows if I decided to snuggle up on him before or after he fell asleep.

I lay still for a while, taking in how nice it feels to be this close to Rio. At the same time it kind of feels wrong because I'm not sure if he would want this or not. The digital clock that sits on the television stand tells me it's already nine in the morning, which means Bronny and Monster will probably be getting up soon, so I decide to sit up carefully, trying not to disturb Rio in the process. The last thing I want is for Rio's roommates to think something is going on when it's not.

Even though I try my hardest not to jostle Rio, it's hard to accomplish since his arm is resting on my waist. When I finally get into a seated position, he begins to move. He blinks at me a couple of times before stretching his arms above his head, which causes his shirt to lift. I get a glimpse at a sliver of skin and neatly trimmed hair that leaves my mouth watering and has me wanting to see more.

Fuck, staying for the second movie was a mistake. I was only trying to be a good friend but now my sleepy brain is thinking of things it shouldn't.

"Looks like we fell asleep," I murmur while trying to discreetly adjust my morning wood.

"You fell asleep ten minutes into the second movie," Rio reminds me before letting out a big yawn. "And I think it only took you another five minutes before you were cuddling up on to my lap."

I grimace a little before whispering my apology, but Rio doesn't look upset and waves me off.

"Nothing to be sorry for." He tilts his head from side to side. "Clearly, you had the right idea about laying down. Who knew sleeping upright would give you this bad of a neck crick."

"Why didn't you go to bed after the movie was done?" I ask, leaning my head slightly to the side, studying him for a moment.

Rio shrugs and glances away, his cheeks turning a rosy shade. "You looked too peaceful. I didn't want to disturb you," he admits, making my heart warm.

"You didn't have to do that," I tell him in a soft voice.

He looks back at me with his lips pressed together. "It's what friends do," he repeats my words from last night back to me while staring at me with a look of longing in his eyes. "Or maybe it's more than that."

My eyebrows shoot up at his admission, and I'm stunned silent for the first time in a long time.

Slowly, like magnets are attached to our lips, we both lean

toward each other. My heart races so fast that it makes it hard to breathe or think about anything except what is about to happen. I'm going to kiss Rio. Something I've dreamt about doing a million times before but also thought would never happen in real life.

We are so close now that I can feel his breath on my skin, but just as we are about to bridge the final gap, a door opening startles us and kills the moment. Rio quickly pulls back and stands so fast I'm surprised he's not lightheaded.

"Shit, I'm sorry," he murmurs before racing down the hall. Leaving me alone in the dimly light living room.

I take a shaky breath before standing, unsure of what just happened. Rio's sudden shock and disappearance stings a little, but I try not to let it get to me. I know that he's demisexual, and maybe he's just realizing that he might have feelings for me. I hope he has feelings for me.

I bet that would be a shock to anyone and I understand him needing time to get his head around it all.

I fish my phone out of my pocket and fire off a message to Rio to make sure we don't end up with awkward feelings from this almost kiss before leaving his apartment and making my way home.

I never thought that kissing Rio would be a real-life possibility, but now that I know that it is, I'm dying to know what it would feel like for it to actually happen.

# CHAPTER TWELVE

MY HEART RACES like a horse on a track as I pace the floor of my bedroom.

I almost kissed Sasha. I *really* wanted to kiss Sasha, but then I heard someone and panicked. And now I feel confused and a bit like an ass. I wonder how Sasha is feeling after I ditched him like that. I start turning to walk back.

The buzzing of my phone pulls me from my panicky state, and I pull it out to check the message.

> Sasha: I guess I've never actually told you this before, but I like you. I'm sorry that our almost kiss scared you. If you want to go out on a date sometime and see if there is something between us more than friendship let me know. If you don't respond I'll just assume it was a sleepy mistake and I'll forget it happened. Everything will go back to normal and there will be no hard feelings. I just didn't want to leave you wondering how I felt.

My body is frozen as I stare at my phone, reading the message over and over again.

Sasha likes me.

I mean, I had my suspicions from time to time, but he's a flirt, so I didn't think it actually meant anything. And he said he wanted to go on a date, which means I really mean something to him, because he doesn't date. He fucks and moves on to the next. Which isn't something I would be comfortable with doing. But is dating Sasha a smart move?

I'm spiraling when my phone vibrates again, but this time, it's a message from BooBoo and not another from Sasha. This leaves me feeling conflicted. I want Sasha to send another message and tell me how much he likes me and why he suddenly wants to date me.

> BooBoo: My mom asked if you are free today for a tarot reading.

Maybe the cards will be able to tell me what I should be doing.

> Me: Sure. What time?

> BooBoo: I can pick you up in an hour.

> Me: Sounds good.

I shove the phone back in my pocket and take a deep breath when I suddenly remember my dream from last night. It was the typical dream of me running, but it wasn't a koala chasing me this time. It was Sasha. Which I guess makes sense. I'm definitely afraid of the feelings I've been having for him, especially since I wasn't sure if he was on the same page. But for some reason, knowing he feels the same doesn't ease my fear.

Letting out a sigh, I throw myself onto my bed and stare at the ceiling.

Why does life have to be so fucking complicated?

EXACTLY ONE HOUR later BooBoo is at my place, and I climb into his car, ready to meet his mom.

"Saying my mom is eccentric would be an understatement," BooBoo states as he drives us to his parents' house. "She's honestly crazy, but she's so loving and kind that it makes up for her weirdness."

I chuckle. "I'm sure she's fine. Aren't all kids supposed to think their parents are weird?"

BooBoo shrugs. "Maybe… But she's like *extra* weird. I just don't want you to say I didn't warn you."

"Dude, I'm going to her for a tarot reading. I know what I'm getting into here."

He hums his acknowledgment. "I guess you're right. Is there anything you're hoping to get from your reading?"

I flip the quartz he gave me in my hand a couple of times before responding. "Clarity, I guess. I don't think this rock is doing that for me."

"Why do you keep carrying it around then?" he questions with a stupid smirk on his lips.

"Because I don't want to tempt shit either. I'm worried if I stop carrying it around shit is going to hit the fan, and I don't want that."

BooBoo laughs, but he knows exactly what I'm talking about. Athletes aren't stereotyped as superstitious for no reason.

The rest of the drive is quick, and my palms start to sweat as we pull into a driveway for a cute little house. Flowers line the sidewalk and a wreath of lavender sits front and center on the door.

"Ready for the weirdness?" BooBoo whispers before opening the door and shouting, "We're here."

"About time," a woman in a flowy dress with long raven

hair says before pulling BooBoo in for a hug. When she lets him go, she turns to me and offers me the brightest smile I've ever seen. It instantly eases the majority of my anxiety. "You must be Rio."

I nod. "And you're BooBoo's mom."

She giggles and grabs my hand. "I am, but you can call me Karla. Come on, I've got everything set up."

Karla gently pulls on my hand, and I follow her to a room that smells like a garden and is filled with herbs and plants. Beside the big bay window, a table is set up with a black tablecloth and a couple of boxes on top. There are two chairs, one on either side of the table.

"Have a seat and pick a tarot deck," she instructs before telling BooBoo to go help his father in the backyard. He stomps off, clearly unexcited with his new task.

Karla lights some incense while I look at the boxes. I'm not sure what the aroma is, but it's somewhat sweet and wraps around me like a blanket of calm. My eyes keep coming back to one box, and I feel like it's calling me, so I tap it, and Karla smiles.

"My simplest of decks," she tells me while putting the other boxes away. "Are you a simple man?"

I shrug. "I guess you could say that."

She hums, then removes the cards from the box and starts to shuffle them. "Have you ever had your cards read before?"

I shake my head. "I've always thought stuff like this was made up," I admit, making her snicker.

"I've heard that plenty of times before. I was like you once," she tells me, and when I narrow my brows at her in my skepticism, it only makes her laugh. "When I was your age, I didn't believe in magic or the spirit world. I thought it was all garbage until my last year of university.

"My roommate for that year was this vibrant young woman who was a firm believer, and I thought she was insane." As Karla talks, cards fly out of her hand, but she doesn't move them, just continues with her story like nothing happened. "She didn't care what I thought about her but asked if she could read my cards one day, and since I was bored, I agreed, thinking nothing would come of it."

"I'm guessing something did come of it?" I check, and she dips her chin with a wide grin.

"Everything the cards predicted came true and it opened up my mind to listening to her more. I realized that what I quickly wrote off as crazy wasn't that at all. Now, it's not going to be for everyone, but I've learned that if we are less judgmental, the world is a much better place. All you need is an open mind or heart. Sometimes, even if your mind is closed, your heart can be open, and the cards will resonate with you."

I know my mind is leery of all of this, but I think my heart is open. Hopefully, that means something will resonate with me during this reading.

There are five cards on the table now, and she stops shuffling to look at them.

"Ready to see what the spirits have in mind for you?" she checks, and I swallow before nodding.

The first card she flips is one that has something that looks like a compass in the middle and gold creatures with wings on each corner. At the bottom, there is writing that says *Wheel of Fortune.*

Karla hums but doesn't offer any words before flipping the second card. This time, the card has a man and a woman standing side by side with an angel hovering over them. On one side of the card, there is also an apple tree with a serpent coiled around it. The words beneath this one are *the lovers.*

The third card she flips shows what looks like a dove diving into a gold cup and is apparently called *The Ace of Cups.*

The fourth card has two people facing each other, each

holding gold cups. At the top is a red lion head with wings. The writing tells me this card is *The Two of Cups*.

The final card she flips has me gasping. But Karly shakes her head with a smile. "Don't fret."

"The card says *death*," I bark out. "How am I not supposed to fret?"

"Things aren't always literal," she assures me as I stare at the card.

There is a skeleton in a knight's outfit on top of a white horse with red eyes. Beneath the horse are dead bodies, and in front of the horse is someone offering a head to the horse. It's creepy, to say the least, and if it doesn't literally mean death then what does it mean?

"We start off your reading with *Wheel of Fortune*, which represents change, and we end with *Death, which* also can mean change or the end of a cycle. Together *Wheel of Fortune* and *Death* encourage us to embrace change and let go of what no longer serves us. They are bookending your other three cards, which *all* have to do with love. Do you have a new love interest in your life?" I press my lips together but eventually nod. "Could they have something to do with why you were having the dreams about running?"

"I think so. Last night, it wasn't the koala chasing me it was Sasha. He's actually the new mascot for GSU, which could make sense as to why the koala was chasing me in the first place."

Karla hums her agreement. "That would make a lot of sense. How come you are afraid of a relationship?"

"I don't really have a lot of experience with dating, and Sasha is known for being a player. I'm afraid that if we try something, it will blow up, and it could wreck the friendship circle we have built. I'm also afraid that if I let him in, he'll end up hurting me."

Karla nods with a soft smile. "I think what the cards are

trying to tell you is to embrace this and let go of your fears. That this relationship is what is meant for you, for right now. I'll be honest and tell you it might not last forever, but I do have a strong belief that it will be good for you for however long it lasts."

Her words resonate with me, but the fear still sits heavy in my gut. I guess the cards aren't able to get rid of that fear for me.

"If you push aside your fear and embrace this new love I see great happiness for you, and isn't that what we all want?" Karla questions, and I nod.

"Thank you for this," I tell her, pushing my chair back and standing.

"Anytime," she assures me and places her hands on my shoulders once she's also come to a stand. "You are worthy of love and happiness. Anything your heart desires."

Her words are like a salve to my heart, and I nod again because I can't think of what else to say.

Karla guides me to the backyard, where BooBoo is helping his dad cut firewood.

"As much as I *love* manual labor, I think it's time for me to go," BooBoo tells his dad once he sees me.

I chuckle and Karla shakes her head. "Come visit soon," she tells me before my friend grabs my arm and ushers me out of their house.

"Dude, I didn't think my mom was going to put me to work today, or I never would have offered to bring you," he grumbles when we get in the car.

"What were you expecting to do?" I question.

"Listen in on your tarot reading, obviously," he responds like it's a no brainer. "Did you find out anything cool?"

"Kind of," I mumble. Apparently, the key to my happiness is to get over my fears and accept change."

BooBoo lets out a full belly laugh at my words. "How come that sounds exactly like most of my readings?"

I can't help but laugh along and shrug. "It's kind of life, isn't it? If only it wasn't easier said than done."

"Tell me about it," BooBoo mumbles, keeping his focus on the road.

The drive home is just as quick as the drive there, but my head isn't any more clear, which kind of sucks. I was wanting clarity in my reading, and all I got was more things to think about.

"Good luck on facing your fears," BooBoo says when he drops me off.

"Thanks," I reply before slowly heading toward my apartment.

Is my true happiness really as easy as pushing my fears aside and letting Sasha in? It can't be that simple, can it? Should I just respond to Sasha's text and see what happens? Maybe things are that easy.

# CHAPTER THIRTEEN

Sasha

THERE IS a giant smile on my face as I'm changing out of my Kerrington Koala costume. I was able to celebrate another win with the GSU soccer team, and the energy from the crowd tonight was electric. I'm so happy I was able to witness the win tonight, especially after the loss the team experienced on Friday. I'm glad they were able to turn it around. Not only did they win, but they played a killer game. I know everyone is proud of them and are excited about being back on track to compete for a potential championship.

"Can I talk with you for a minute?" Evangeline asks when I step out of the changing room.

"Of course, what's up?" I ask, leaning against the wall.

"I know when we hired you, I told you that you'd be a part of a lot of different sporting events, but Coach Rudder has requested a change," she tells me. My stomach drops.

"They hate me?" I question, feeling like an utter failure.

"Oh my God, no," she quickly corrects me. "They *love* you, so much so that the team has developed a superstition around you. They've asked that you attend *all* of their games. We don't normally have a mascot at every soccer game, but it's hard to convince athletes that superstitions aren't real. Logistically, it's probably going to be a nightmare to work it out, but with how well the team was playing up until their last game, there is a strong chance they are going to bring home the championship win. But they won't be able to do that if the team is stuck in their head thinking they'll only win if you are there."

I blink at her a couple of times. "So, I'm not fired?" I check and she laughs.

"No, but you are going to be a bit busier than we originally thought."

After my training was complete, I was supposed to go around and fill in for the other mascots, but apparently, that won't be happening anymore. Which isn't something I'm going to complain about. I'll get to be at every single one of Rio's games and get to ogle him from the sidelines. And if he ever decides to ask me out on that date, then things will be even better. We won't have to spend a ton of time apart while trying to build a relationship. Of course, that's all just wishful thinking at this point in time. It's not like he's texted me to say he wants to try something, and we haven't really seen each other since the night we almost kissed.

"I'm cool with being busy," I tell her with a smile. "I might have to talk to a couple of my professors though to make sure it's okay for me to miss a class here and there as I'm not sure the away games line up with my current schedule."

Evangeline nods. "How 'bout we sit down with your schedule, and I'll email any professor you need me to. They tend to be more willing to be flexible if it comes from someone higher up than a student."

"Thank you."

"Thank *you* for being so understanding. Thankfully, we have the two mascot costumes, but a third would be really handy right about now."

"Maybe the school will find some random funding and gift it to you," I say, which makes her laugh.

"And maybe pigs will fly," she retorts.

"True, but weirder things have happened," I explain.

She shrugs. "True story, keep your fingers crossed. In the meantime, get ready for an away game Friday."

"I'm always ready," I tell her with a wink before making my way down the hall with an extra pep in my step.

WEDNESDAY AND THURSDAY pass by in a blur and before I know it Friday is here. I'm both excited and extremely nervous to be traveling with the soccer team for their away game.

On one hand, I'm excited to see Rio and the guys play, but on the other, I'm anxious that they'll lose and blame it on me. I'm supposed to be their good luck charm, and it will destroy me if I can't be that for them. The pressure is real.

"Want to be seat buddies?" Rio asks when I arrive at the bus, causing my brows to shoot up in shock.

He hasn't asked me out yet so I'm trying my hardest to pretend like last weekend didn't happen, but it's kind of hard.

"Umm, yeah, that would be cool," I somewhat stutter over my words.

"Awesome. I've been wanting to talk to you, but life has been busy. I'm glad you're our full-time mascot now," he tells me, and butterflies erupt in my stomach.

What could he possibly want to talk about? Is he finally going to ask me out? Is he going to thank me for acting like last weekend never happened?

A million possible scenarios run through my head as I follow Rio onto the bus.

"Hey, you're supposed to sit with me," BooBoo complains when Rio and I take our seats. "I thought we were bus besties."

"Just because we always sit together doesn't mean I'm *only* allowed to sit with you," Rio retorts.

BooBoo grumbles and takes the seat in front of us. "I feel like I'm being cheated on."

Rio chuckles. "You'll always be my favorite even if I don't sit with you," he assures him.

"Does that mean you're going to tell me how you got your nickname?" BooBoo asks, looking over the back of his chair at us.

Rio shakes his head with a shit-eating grin. "Absolutely not."

"I think we should choose a new nickname for you since apparently no one even knows how you got it anymore," BooBoo complains.

"If you can come up with something better, be my guest," Rio offers.

BooBoo glares at him for a moment before huffing and turning around again.

"No one knows how you got your nickname?" I check, and Rio shakes his head with a smirk.

"Obviously, there are a few who do, but it's been so long that the majority have forgotten. Honestly, most people don't even ask about it anymore. They just accept that I go by Rio and leave it at that."

I nod but my mind starts racing at what the story could possibly be. It must be something crazy embarrassing if he won't tell anyone how he got the nickname. I wonder what I would have to do to get him to tell me the story. Gossip is an addiction for me, and this feels like something I would absolutely love to hear.

"I've been thinking about your text," Rio says once the bus starts moving and people are caught up in their own conversations.

"Really?" I check.

"Yeah, but I'll admit I was a little confused."

"What about? I thought I was pretty straightforward," I tell him.

"You were, but I'm just confused why you want to date me. You aren't the dating type. I've known you for what, three years? And I've never seen you date anyone. Sleep with people? Yes. But never date. Why the change in heart?"

I nibble on my lower lip as I think about my answer.

Rio isn't wrong. I don't date. Haven't since my last relationship that I literally ran away from after I almost died at the hands of the man who was supposed to love me. Dating *anyone* has been the last thing I've wanted to do. Well, until I got to know Rio. I realized that if I was to ever date again, I would want it to be with a man like him. He was always so kind, and he didn't fall for my overt flirting. I liked that I always had to try harder with him. Rio is different than any guy I've ever met, and even though it's been a long time since I've had a boyfriend, I know I could be a good one for him. And there's no doubt in my mind that he'll treat me better than my ex.

"I haven't had the best history with dating," I admit in a quiet voice. "The last relationship I was in was toxic, to say the least, and I've been terrified to share my heart with anyone ever since."

"My question still remains. Why the change?"

"When I met you, I thought you were so hot that I was afraid you were going to set me on fire," I admit, making Rio blush a little, and he shoves me with his shoulder. "But no matter how hard I flirted, you never took the bait."

"Because I'm demi," he reminds me, and I nod.

"But I didn't know that at the time. Eventually, I just figured you weren't interested, which was fine with me because it was just as much fun to tease you. As I got to know you more and spend time with you, I got to see what a great guy you are. You have this grumpy exterior at times, or maybe aloof is a better word, either way, you are tough on the outside but soft on the inside," I ramble, rushing the words out. "You don't let that side out all the time, but when you do, it's enough to make me melt every time."

"My crush on you started to grow and morph. I no longer wanted you to just fuck my brains out. I wanted to spend more time with you, to hold your hand and cuddle. For the first time since my breakup, I wanted a relationship. I just didn't think you wanted that with me. So, I stuck to teasing you and being your annoying friend."

"For a while, I didn't even know if we were friends," Rio admits. "I thought of you as more of an annoying acquaintance at the beginning."

Some might take offense to what Rio just told me, but in all honesty, I see where he's coming from. I *do come* across strong when I want someone. And even though with most people, I settle down quickly after rejection, I didn't with him because he was too much fun to tease. I enjoyed making him blush and getting him all flustered, and he never flat out told me to stop.

"But eventually, as I got to know you, I found out there was more to you than meets the eye," he tells me. "You can be sweet and caring, and your flirting is just a facade. There are layers to you, and I've enjoyed seeing every side of you that you've shown to me."

I'm not one to blush easily, but my cheeks heat at his sweet words.

"I'd like to see even more of you," he whispers, and his confession almost makes it hard to breathe.

"Are you saying you want to date me?" I check, and he presses his lips together before nodding.

"I want to be honest that I'll need to take things slow, but I want to see where this can go."

"I'm not known for going slow," I remind him. "But I can take this as slow as you need me to. I'm just excited that you're actually willing to try this."

"I'll admit that I'm a little terrified, but I've been told that sometimes we have to push our fears aside to let in the happiness we deserve."

I smile, and I'm itching to grab his hand, but I want him to make the first move. Moving at a glacier pace isn't my usual way, so for the time being, I need Rio to take the lead. If he's in charge, I won't be tempted to push things too far.

"Thank you for taking a chance on me. I'll try not to let you down." A hint of insecurity creeps up as I let the words out.

What if my last relationship was a failure because of me? I know my therapist told me that no matter what I did it would never warrant the way Lux treated me, but it's hard to believe that sometimes. Maybe I'm only good for sex, and I'm doomed to never be loved the way I've always desired. I know Rio will never do the things Lux did, but what if he decides I'm not a good enough boyfriend for him? He said he wants to see more of me, but what if I show him the sides of myself that I keep hidden from everyone, then decides he wants someone else?

Rio grabs my hand, giving it a squeeze and pulling me from my internal downward spiral. "There is nothing you could do to let me down," he tells me with a certainty in his voice. "I can't see the future to know if this relationship will work out, but if something happens, it won't be because you did anything wrong. It will be because we weren't meant to be, but we'll never know if we don't try."

I take a shaky breath and plaster on a smile. "Have you always been this wise?" I joke, and he chuckles.

"Not really, but I met someone recently who has opened my eyes to a lot of things."

Rio fiddles with something in his free hand and my eyes go wide when I see that it's a clear quartz.

"Since when are you a crystal kind of guy?" I question.

"Since I started having weird dreams, BooBoo's mom

insisted that I carry this around with me. Are you into rocks too?"

I chuckle, trying not to take offense that he just called them rocks, and nod as I hold up the necklace I never take off. "This is amethyst," I tell him, and he grabs onto the amulet to study it more. "Amethyst is known for its ability to protect and provide stress relief. I wear it to repel negative energy. My mom was all about crystals and taught me a lot about them."

"That's cool. I bet your mom and BooBoo's mom would have gotten along well."

"Are you talking about my mom?" BooBoo asks, turning around in his seat, clearly hearing the last of what Rio said.

"Sasha's mom was into rocks too," Rio tells him.

"That's cool," he says with a smile. "Want to introduce the two? My mom loves meeting like-minded people."

Rio clears his throat and when I turn to him, he's glaring at his friend.

"What?" BooBoo questions with furrowed brows.

"My mom passed away," I tell him, and his face immediately falls.

"Shit. I'm so sorry. I heard it *was,* but it didn't click. I'm such a dick."

I wave him off. "It's fine. My mom might not be able to meet yours, but I can. I'd love to see her crystal collection."

"Oh, she's totally going to love you," BooBoo says, his smile finally returning. "If you want, I can give her your number and she can set up something with you. But just know I'm not sticking around this time. I don't need to get roped into *more* chores. I moved out so I wouldn't have to do them anymore."

Rio snickers. "I went over for a tarot reading, and BooBoo's dad made him chop firewood," he informs me.

"My arms were like Jell-O the next day," BooBoo complains.

"You weren't even there that long," Rio states. "You're just being a baby."

BooBoo sticks his tongue out at Rio, and I laugh, but my thoughts are stuck on what Rio said a moment ago.

"You got a tarot reading?" I ask. Rio does not seem like the type to be open to things like that. But I guess he *is* carrying around a crystal.

"I did," he says with a dip of his chin. "I'll admit I'm still skeptical about it, but the cards were interesting and insightful."

"Now I totally have to meet your mom," I tell BooBoo. "I haven't had my cards read in forever. I used to have my own deck, but I lost it when I broke up with my ex and haven't bought a new one."

I lost some faith in my spirit guides after everything that went down with Lux, so I didn't feel like replacing a lot of my stuff, which is silly, I know.

It's been years since he's been out of my life, and even though I vowed he wouldn't have control over me anymore, he clearly still does, which is the last thing I want.

"Now I'm nervous about introducing you to my mom. She's probably going to love you more than me," BooBoo jokes.

"I am very loveable. I mean, your team loves me so much that I'm stuck being your personal mascot," I reply with a toothy grin.

BooBoo laughs. "Touché. Here, put your number in, and I'll send it to my mom. Expect a text from her soon," he says, handing me his phone.

I do as I'm told, then give him his phone back, and he sits properly in his seat again.

"Does it scare you that I'm into crystals, essential oils, and tarot cards?" I check with Rio, and he shakes his head.

"Not at all. I'm honestly not surprised you're into that kind of stuff."

"Want to tell me what your reading was like?" I check, more than a little intrigued when Rio blushes at the question.

"Not yet," he replies quietly.

"You know they aren't like wishes. Telling someone won't affect whether they come true or not," I tell him, and he shrugs.

"I guess I just want to wait a little longer," he says.

"I can respect that. I remember sometimes needing time to process what the cards were telling me. But if you ever want to talk about it, or anything, I'm here."

He smiles and I almost swoon at just how gorgeous he is when his face lights up like that.

"I think there is going to be lots of talking about a bunch of different things in our future. That's what dating is all about, isn't it?"

Butterflies flutter in my stomach at the mention of dating, and I nod.

I can't believe I'm dating Rio. It's like my dreams are finally coming true. Let's just hope I don't do anything to mess things up.

# CHAPTER FOURTEEN

THE SMILE I'm sporting is so big that it almost hurts. I'm pretty sure there's nothing that could wipe it off my face, and I'm willing to deal with sore cheeks if it means I get to keep feeling this high.

"Is there a certain koala that has you grinning like that?" BooBoo asks as we change. I flip him the bird but don't deny his statement. "Are you guys dating now?"

"I asked him out on the bus," I admit.

"That's awesome, dude. You deserve to be happy."

"Thanks, man," I reply as Coach walks in to give us our pre-game pep talk.

In what feels like no time at all, we're heading out to the pitch, ready to take on our competition on their home turf. I know more than a few of us are nervous after our last away game loss, but when I see Sasha on the sidelines in his Kerrington costume, my worries fade, and I hope my teammates feel the same.

I'm sure it seems stupid to people that we feel like the only way we'll win is with Kerrington on the sidelines, and maybe it is, but superstitions don't need to make sense for people to believe them. And our team has it in our heads that he's the key to our victory. Thankfully, Coach was able to convince Evangeline that we need the koala mascot because otherwise, this season would be over before it started.

Whether or not Kerrington actually brings us good luck doesn't matter. If the majority of our players think he does, they'll get all up in their heads if he isn't here for us and play like shit.

When I look up at the crowd, I'm not surprised that our fan section is a lot smaller. The farther we travel for games, the fewer people we have cheering us on, which makes sense since it's not easy for everyone to travel to all of our games. Thankfully, those who have shown up tonight are loud and doing their best to make up for the lack of numbers.

Kerrington is dancing on the sidelines, getting the crowd going as we get into position, and my smile grows even wider. Not only do we have our good luck charm with us tonight, but I'm also dating him, and that makes it even more special. I'm determined to play my absolute best tonight, not only to make our fans proud but to show the guy I like how talented our team is.

When we win, I might just earn myself a congratulations kiss. I haven't been able to stop thinking about Sasha's lips since our almost kiss last weekend. Are they as soft as they look? Is he a pliant kisser who will let me take the lead or is he more dominant, preferring to be in control? Does he like to use his tongue or teeth? Would he let his hands roam over my body? What would they feel like?

I shake my head since now is not the time to think about those things. My focus needs to be on the game. Once the game is over, I can daydream —or better yet, I can make those dreams come true.

I narrow my eyes at my opponents, taking a deep inhale and tuning out the outside world like I always do. All that matters right now is soccer and bringing home another win for GSU.

THE GAME GOES by in a sweaty blur, and I'm almost caught off guard when the crowd starts counting down. The ball is in my possession, and I dribble it down the pitch with lightning speed, dodging my opponents as I go. I keep my eyes open to see if any of my teammates are available for me to pass to, but everyone is guarded at the moment, so I keep my feet moving. At the last moment, I fake like I'm about to pass to BooBoo, who is somewhat open, before moving in the opposite direction and kicking the ball with all my might. Sending it soaring into the net.

I'm tackled to the ground by BooBoo, and not even a second later, Whiley piles on top of him, shouting his enthusiasm.

"What a fucking game!" BooBoo yells as we celebrate our victory.

"I told you Kerrington was our lucky mascot," Whiley says as the aforementioned koala joins us to celebrate our win. "I'm willing to fight anyone who tries to take him away from us."

Kerrington does a couple of back flips before high fiving the guys he passes as he runs around the pitch. The poor cheerleader who is supposed to be his handler struggles to keep up with him but he clearly doesn't care about the possibility of tripping. When he gets to me, he holds my arm up like he's done most of our games but this time instead of feeling embarrassed I feel excited.

"Did you see us destroy them?" I ask the koala, who nods his head.

There's no way fans could hear him if he spoke, but Sasha is a professional and keeps quiet like he was trained to do. For some reason, I don't need to hear him speak. His presence alone covers me in warmth and comfort. It's a weird feeling but one I really enjoy.

"There is a young fan who wants to meet you," Hailey

tells Sasha, who nods, then waves at us, throws his arms up in celebration one more time, then follows the cheerleader.

I watch as Sasha kneels in front of a young boy who's smiling so wide I can't help but grin myself. I'm forced to tear my gaze away from them just after they high-five as it's time to get to the locker room to change and hear what Coach has to say. I should want to shower off the sweat and grime from my body but it's hard to get my feet to move. I don't think I've ever been this into someone that I struggle to take my eyes off them, even for a short amount of time.

"Come on," BooBoo says, grabbing my arm and pulling me off the field. "You can hang out with your boyfriend later. Besides, he's busy doing his job right now."

I sigh but nod and let my friend guide me to where I need to be.

Who knew I would be this crazy about Sasha so soon? But the even crazier part is I'm not that scared about it.

I'm embracing the new in my life like the tarot cards said to, and that alone is helping ease my fears, leaving my heart open to the love the cards promised.

# CHAPTER FIFTEEN

**"YOU'RE THE BEST MASCOT EVER,"** Thomas, the little boy who was so eager to meet me, says with a toothy grin. "Can you do another backflip for me?"

"Thomas, Kerrington isn't a show pony," his father reminds the child, but I wave him off and step back to show off my moves, which has the boy smiling brightly and laughing with pure joy.

"Unfortunately, that's all the time we have tonight, but hopefully, you can come to more games in the future," Hailey tells the boy when I'm done.

He nods quickly like a little bobblehead. "My dad is the soccer fan, but Kerrington is the reason I come. I've never seen a mascot move like he does."

"Thomas wasn't looking forward to this weekend since he thinks his grandparent's house is boring, but when I told him we could come to this game his entire attitude changed. I'm just glad you were here. I know the mascots aren't always at away games."

"Kerrington will be at every GSU soccer game this season," Hailey informs them, and the boy's face lights up.

"Looks like I'll need to buy more tickets," the father says while smiling at his son.

I give Thomas another high-five before letting Hailey guide me to our change area.

"You need to slow down on the field after the games," Hailey says as she helps me take the koala head off.

"Why?" I question with a raised brow. "Do you struggle to keep up?"

She rolls her eyes at my playfulness. "How you move as fast as you do in that fucking thing, I will never understand. But what I was really trying to get at with my statement is if you run off on me like that, there is a higher chance you'll fall and get hurt. I know you can't see much in that thing which is why you have a handler in the first place. The last thing we want is for you to get injured and not be able to perform. You know how superstitious the team is. If you're down and out so will the team be."

I sigh, but it's hard to fight logic like that.

"Fine, I'll slow down or at least give you a run-down of my plan before bolting onto the pitch," I assure her.

She smiles and nods. "That's all I ask. I know the fans love seeing your energy, but I'm serious when I say it would be the end of the world if you get injured. GSU wants the championship win this year, and that won't be possible if the team loses their good luck charm."

"I've never understood how superstitious athletes can be," I mumble as I open a water bottle and guzzle down the contents, remembering Gabriel telling me about how Chase only washes his socks on the first of the month.

"It's exhausting sometimes," Hailey says. "I've seen the dumbest shit happen all over a stupid superstition. Sometimes I also think people make shit up just so they'll be treated special."

"Like what?" I ask as she helps me out of the rest of the costume.

"One player for the football team last year told everyone he had to have sex the night before a game," she explains, and I gasp at the audacity of the man. She giggles before continuing. "The thing is, even though I thought he was lying, there was a game that apparently he didn't get laid before, and they lost so badly it almost hurt."

"Damn," I whisper before Hailey darts behind a curtained off area to get changed.

Since it's just the two of us, I stay where I am and work quickly to get out of my sweaty clothes and change into clean dry ones. I'll shower at the hotel later tonight since our room doesn't have showers.

"Are you decent?" Hailey asks before coming out from behind the curtain.

"My junks covered," I call out, and she giggles before joining me in the open space.

"I'm glad I got assigned to be your main handler," she tells me with a big grin. "You're a lot more fun than the others on the mascot team."

"I've barely met them," I tell her as I pull my shirt on and gather up my belongings. "I've been busy focusing on my training with Evangeline and have only met each of them once. Now that I'm dedicated to the soccer team, I probably won't see them at all."

I know that if I was switching off, I'd have to meet with the mascot team to give them a brief breakdown of what went down, but since I won't be doing that, I can skip that step.

"Well, between you and me, you're the best," she tells me with a wink.

I chuckle and shake my head. "You don't need to butter me up I already love you," I tell her then tilt my head toward the bags for the mascot costume. "Think we can convince some of the players to help us carry Kerrington?"

"I bet Rio would be on board," she says with a knowing smirk. "I saw you two talking on the bus and looking all cozy together. And then after the game, he couldn't take his eyes off of you."

I press my lips together, but I can't contain the grin that's wanting to spread across my lips. "He maybe sort of asked me out," I tell her, feeling like a teenager again.

Hailey squeals, but it's quickly cut off by a knock on the door.

"Did you guys need help?" Rio calls out through the door.

"Did we summon him somehow?" Hailey whispers before letting him and BooBoo in. "We were just talking about needing some muscle to move this stupid costume," she says, batting her eyes at BooBoo, who blushes instantly.

"Well, good thing we decided to stop by," he tells her with a charming grin.

Rio winks at me but doesn't say anything. Instead, he just helps me pack up the costume then him and BooBoo carry the bags out.

"If I knew dating a soccer player would get me out of carrying that heavy thing, I would have tried to do it sooner," I joke as we walk down the hall to the bus.

"I'm also happy I get to cash in on the soccer boyfriend perks," Hailey voices.

"Want your own soccer boyfriend?" BooBoo asks.

"I don't know, I think all the good-looking players are taken now," she says with a pout.

"I'm single," he tells her, completely missing the joke she just made.

"I stand by the statement I just said," Hailey says with a sassy tone and winks at him before climbing onto the bus.

BooBoo stands there for a moment with his jaw damn near on the floor. "Did she just call me ugly?"

I laugh and shrug. "Maybe she's playing hard to get?"

BooBoo presses his lips together and nods before placing his part of the mascot costume beneath the bus. "Well, it's a good thing I like a challenge," he grumbles before following Hailey on board.

"Those two would make a cute couple," I tell Rio as he puts the bags he was carrying beneath the bus.

"Hailey would be good for him. BooBoo needs a woman who will put him in his place," he replies as we take the steps into the bus and find two open seats. "Are you rooming with Hailey tonight?"

I nod. "Evangeline made sure it was okay with the both of us, but since I'm gay, Hailey said she didn't have any concerns that I would come on to her."

Rio laughs. "She makes a solid point."

"Why are you asking? Would you like to come over and visit?" I check.

"Yeah. I was kind of hoping that I earned a victory kiss. I'm still kicking myself in the ass for not following through last weekend."

My heart beats a little faster at his confession, and my body heats with desire. "Is BooBoo your roommate? Maybe we can convince Hailey to hang out with him for a little bit."

Rio bites his lower lip and nods. "I like that idea."

Holy shit. If things go according to plan, I'm going to be alone with Rio, which has happened many times in the past, but tonight will be different. It will be the first time we're alone together since we've decided to try things. I can't wait to kiss him and see where the night takes us. To some, it might be fast and feel like we're skipping steps like not actually going on a first date, but it doesn't feel rushed to me. Maybe it's because we've been friends for so long.

"BooBoo invited me to his room to play video games with him," Hailey tells me when we get to the hotel room. "So, you'll have our room all to yourself until curfew." She winks at me, and I instantly pull her into my arms for a bear hug.

"You are the best friend a boy could ask for," I whisper into her ear.

"I know," she sing-songs. "Now be a dear and take my bag to our room," she tells me before handing over her rolling bag.

"If this is the price I have to pay to spend some time alone with a guy I like, then I'll gladly pay it," I say as the boys join us.

"I hear Hailey and BooBoo are going to hang out for a bit," Rio tells me with excitement in his eyes when he stares at me.

"Meet me at my room in fifteen minutes," I reply as we get on the elevator.

"Why can't I come now?" he asks, tilting his head to the side.

"Because I need to shower," I tell him. "Our change area didn't have one, and I *need* to wash this sweat off me."

"I can appreciate that," he replies with a dip of his chin. "But I'll be knocking on your door in exactly fifteen minutes. I'm really looking forward to that celebratory kiss."

"Aww, they are too cute together," Hailey coos, leaning into BooBoo a little.

"Can I get a celebratory kiss too?" he asks her, but she only rolls her eyes.

"You have to do more than win a soccer game to earn a kiss from me."

"Can't blame a guy for asking," he mutters.

The elevator opens and I turn to the left as the rest of them turn to the right. I give them a wave before disappearing into my hotel room.

My heart is racing as anticipation for what's about to happen ripples through my body.

I'm finally going to kiss Rio.

# CHAPTER SIXTEEN

MY PALMS ARE clammy as I knock on the door to Sasha's hotel room. I'm beyond nervous to be alone with Sasha, but that's bound to be expected. I'm not a virgin, but since it's harder for me to experience sexual desire than the average person, I feel like an amateur compared to Sasha. Not that we're planning on having sex tonight or anything.

All we've discussed is kissing, but I know that usually leads to more. Is he going to expect more? He said he would be okay with going slow, but is he going to change his mind if things start getting hot and heavy? Is he going to expect things to move at a pace he's more used to? Is he going to be disappointed if I stop things before they get too far?

I'm attracted to Sasha, he turns me on like no one ever has and eventually I might want to go all the way with him, but I know I won't be ready to do that tonight.

"Hey, handsome," Sasha greets me when he opens the door and holds it for me.

I check him out as I pass him, and he closes the door. I very much approve of how he looks. He's wearing a pair of jeans that cling to his legs in the most perfect way, and the black shirt he has on hugs his pectoral muscles. His hair is still wet, leaving wet spots on his shirt in a few places. His skin is flushed from the heat of his shower, and I have to admit it's a good look on him. It makes me want to find ways to keep that flush there.

"Like what you see," Sasha asks after I'm done my perusal of him.

I lick my lips and nod. "You know how hot you are."

He shrugs. "Yes, but I never get tired of hearing it."

I step toward him and place my hand on his waist. "You are so fucking sexy," I whisper. "And I'm dying to kiss those delectable lips."

"Then do it," he encourages me, and I close the distance between us, finally doing what I've been wanting to do for the past six days.

The kiss starts out tentative as I gently press my lips to his, savoring how soft they are. He lets me take the lead, exploring his mouth. I give him a few pecks before licking the seam of his lips. A throaty moan ripples past his lips as he opens them for me, allowing me to deepen the kiss.

My hands slowly start to roam up and down his back as we make out, and my cock pushes against my underwear every time he whimpers or moans. I swallow down all of his noises, digging how vocal he is.

When I thrust into Sasha's leg, he groans before slowly stepping back, breaking our kiss, leaving us both panting for air.

"I think maybe we should take a break and talk," Sasha suggests, grabbing my hand and guiding me to the bed.

"I think that's a good idea," I reply before sitting beside him on the queen size mattress.

I love that he's helping me keep things slow. As turned on as I am right now, there's a part of me that's wanting to throw caution out the window and jump his bones right here and now. But there is another part of me that will regret that in the morning. I want a relationship, not just a tumble in the sack.

"Tell me something almost no one knows about you," he says with an even smile.

"I have no idea what I'm going to do when I graduate," I tell him, and his brows crinkle together.

"I thought you were going to be a teacher," he responds, and I nod.

"I am, but that's all I know. I don't know where I'm going to live or anything else."

"You don't want to move home?" he inquires.

"I have nothing back there. I mean, my parents are there, but they couldn't care less about me. They weren't abusive, but they were neglectful, and I have no desire to go through that again."

"I'm sorry you had to go through that. Did you have any other family that was better?" he asks.

"I had my grandpa, but he passed away. So now it's just me, and I'm kind of scared to have to make this decision on my own," I whisper.

Sasha rests his hand on my knee and gives it a squeeze. "But you're not alone. You have me, and you also have some amazing friends," he reminds me.

The corners of my lips turn upward, and I put my hand on top of his. "I really needed to hear that."

"Even if our romantic relationship doesn't work out, I'm always going to be your friend," he reassures me.

"I appreciate that. What are your plans after you graduate?"

"I think I'm going to stay in Green Spring," he tells me. "I also don't have any family around. And I will *never* move back to California. Since my friends are all here, it doesn't make sense for me to leave unless I can't find a job."

"You don't miss the warm weather?" I check, earning me a shrug.

"I guess so, but that place holds too many bad memories for me. I don't think I could even visit. I wouldn't feel safe there."

"Do you want to talk about why?" I ask him softly.

Sasha looks up at the ceiling and takes a deep inhale before slowly blowing it out and shaking his head. "Not tonight. I want to one day, but I also don't want to bring the mood down. My past sucks, and it's hard to talk about. Honestly, I haven't talked about it much because of how painful it is to remember."

I smile at him and nod, happy that he told me as much as he did. "I'm here when you're ready," I promise him.

"I appreciate that. How about you tell me how you got your nickname to brighten the mood?" he suggests, shooting me a toothy grin that makes me chuckle.

"Do you want to know why I don't tell the story?" I ask him, and he nods like an eager kid. "Because it's boring and stupid. By not telling it, people think it has to be something epic when in reality, it's lame."

"Well, now you have to tell me," Sasha says, and I sigh.

I'm about to spill the beans when the door flies open. "I'm so sorry," Hailey says while laughing, sprinting into the room completely naked.

"Where the hell are your clothes?" Sasha asks with wide eyes.

"BooBoo dared me to dart down the hall naked," she explains while grabbing her bag and disappearing into the bathroom. She keeps the door cracked open so we can hear her as she continues the story. "I was on my way back to his room when Coach opened his door, and we made eye contact. Thankfully, I was smart enough to grab my keycard for this room before racing down the hall, and I didn't have to run all the way back to BooBoo's room."

Sasha falls back on the bed, cackling. "Oh my god, you are too much."

A loud pounding on the door has me grimacing, but Sasha doesn't seem to be bothered as he walks over to open it.

Coach Rudder is standing there with a very pissed-off expression and a tick in his jaw. "Rio, I think it's time for you to go back to your room," he commands, and I nod slowly, standing. "And Hailey, I better not catch you outside of this room until morning," he shouts so she can hear him.

"Yes, Sir," she replies from the bathroom.

Coach sighs and shakes his head before leaving.

"Well, it looks like our night has been cut short," I reply and pull Sasha toward me for a goodbye kiss.

"Goodbye for now, handsome. I look forward to hearing the story behind your nickname the next time we get together," he tells me with a wink.

I land another peck on his lips before leaving his room and heading to mine.

BooBoo looks up with wide eyes when I enter our room. "Hailey's been grounded thanks to your dare," I tell him, which only makes him laugh.

"I really didn't think she was going to do it, but damn, do I respect the shit out of her now for following through," BooBoo says, and I chuckle along with him before sitting on my bed.

"We know now that she isn't one to turn down a dare."

BooBoo nods. "True story. Sorry about cutting your evening with Sasha short."

I wave him off. "It's all good. We still had a nice time."

"Niiiccee tiiimme, ehhh?" he says, drawing each word out and making me roll my eyes. "How nice are we talking?"

I throw a pillow at him this time but can't help but laugh along with him. "I'm not about to spill the details of my love life, but I will tell you that I got my congratulatory kiss," I tell him.

"Nice. Well, I'm glad one of us got a kiss."

"Are you actually into Hailey or just wanting to have a good time?" I question him and he lifts a shoulder.

"Honestly. I'm not sure. I mean, I wouldn't turn down a horizontal tango with her, but I also don't think I would turn down more. She's really cool, and I enjoyed hanging out with her tonight. I guess I'll just have to play it by ear," he says.

"That is if she forgives you for getting her in trouble with Coach."

BooBoo's eyes go wide. "Shit, you don't think that could have ruined my chances, do you?"

I shrug. "I have no idea, my guy, but she didn't seem upset about getting in shit, so you're probably okay. Just keep the stupid shit to a minimum if you actually want a chance at something with her."

"Yeah, I'll keep that in mind. But if she doesn't hate my guts after that, and we keep the same sleeping arrangements all season, I'd be happy to keep her company while you spend time with your man."

I chuckle and shake my head. "Thanks, I can hear how agonizing that's going to be for you," I tease.

"It will be, but I value our friendship so much that I'm willing to take one for the team."

"You're an idiot," I tell him as we both laugh.

Tonight was amazing, and as much as I enjoyed the kissing and the talking, I can't help but think that we need to go on an actual date. Our next game isn't until next Sunday, so we have lots of time to figure out a night that would work for the both of us. The wheels in my brain are beginning to spin as I think of the perfect date to take Sasha on. I want to show him how a partner should really treat him. Even though he hasn't told me much about his ex, I know that the guy was a fucking tool. He hurt a man who is so full of life and love, and I just don't understand how someone could do that.

I make a silent vow to myself to only ever show Sasha kindness and respect, something his ex should have done but clearly didn't.

# CHAPTER SEVENTEEN

HAILEY and I make our way onto the bus at a snail's pace until Coach Rudder shouts at us to hurry up. Hailey books it down the aisle to find an open seat and avoid Coach's glare. Thankfully, he doesn't say anything about last night, and I take the open seat next to Rio.

"You two were sure running behind this morning," Rio notes as I get comfortable.

"We were up late talking, and we both forgot to set alarms," I murmur, feeling a little embarrassed.

Rio snickers while shaking his head at me. "How come that sounds exactly like you?"

I sigh. "Because it is. Without Evangeline, I'm bound to fall apart sooner or later."

He gives my knee a squeeze, which helps to make me feel a little bit better. "You're new to this kind of life. You'll get used to it," he assures me.

I want to argue, but for some reason, I actually believe him.

"Why are you so confident in me?" I question with a tilt of my head. "You know that my life can be a shit show, and I suck at punctuality. What if I don't get used to it and I eventually get fired?"

"I'm confident in you because I've also seen what you can do when you put your mind to it. And you're not alone in this. I can help you be more punctual. If we both have to be in the same places at the same time, I can be your alarm and make sure you're never late."

"You'd do that for me?" I whisper, and the smile that he offers me damn near turns me into a puddle of mush.

"Of course I will. In case you didn't figure it out last night, I like you, Sasha, and I want to see you shine. If that means giving you friendly reminders here and there, I'll gladly do it. Honestly, I think I would do anything you ask of me."

His confession has more butterflies erupting in my stomach. How did I get so lucky to have a man like this in my life?

"You're too sweet," I whisper while intertwining our fingers and sliding my hand into his.

"You deserve to be treated like this, and I'm sorry if your ex made you think you didn't," he tells me, giving my hand a squeeze. "Speaking of being treated the right way, what are you up to tonight? I'd like to take you out on a proper date."

I can't help from wiggling in my seat with excitement. "Umm, I'm free. Do you have something in mind?" I inquire.

"I do, but I'd like to keep it a surprise if that's okay with you."

The fact that he's asking for permission to surprise me melts my heart. He isn't just assuming I'll be okay with it, and he's giving me a chance to opt-out if I'm not.

"I'm good with a surprise," I tell him, even though I'm dying to know what the plan is. I also know waiting and seeing what he has up his sleeve will be much better.

"Perfect. I'll pick you up at seven. Wear something comfortable and warm."

The wheels in my head start spinning, trying to figure out what he could have possibly planned for us on such short notice.

"Should I eat before you pick me up, or will food be included?" I check.

"I've got food covered," he tells me, and I smile.

"You do know the only thing I'm going to think about the entire drive home now is going to be our date, right?"

Rio chuckles and squeezes my hand. "I'm sorry, but I'm glad you're excited."

Excited doesn't even begin to describe how I'm feeling, but I keep that information to myself. I don't want to come across as too eager, although I'm probably doing a really bad job of not showing just how much I'm looking forward to this date. I'm just excited for us to get to spend more time together and to find out what he's planned.

"Has BooBoo's mom gotten a hold of you yet?" Rio asks as the bus drives us back to Green Spring.

I smile just at the mention of BooBoo's mom, who has already turned out to be an amazing person, and I haven't even met her yet.

"Yes, she's been texting me on and off since yesterday. I can't wait to meet her in person."

"She's awesome. I bet you'll love her. Do you have plans to meet up yet?"

"Yup. I'm heading over there Tuesday afternoon," I tell him with a big smile.

"Awesome. Did you need a ride?" he inquires, and I shrug.

"I was just going to order a ride-share."

He shakes his head. "Why pay the money when I can take you? I don't have anything going on Tuesday afternoon."

"Are you sure?" I ask, hearing the insecurity in my voice.

"I'm sure. And I don't even have to stay if you want time alone with Karla. I'll just drop you off, then pick you up when you're done."

"You'd really do that?" I question, hating that I have so much doubt.

"Babe, I wouldn't offer if I didn't mean it," he assures me. I have a car, and you don't. Even if we weren't dating, I'd still probably offer to drive you. It's what friends do like you told me last weekend when you did my laundry and made me dinner."

When he puts it like that it makes me feel stupid for wondering why he's being like this. This is how someone is *supposed* to treat their partner. Lux was an asshole, and I should have clued in earlier that he wasn't a good guy. But by the time I saw his real colors, it was too late. Although even before Lux let down his façade, he wasn't thoughtful like Rio's being right now. But I was young then, and I didn't know how I should really be treated.

"Well, if you don't mind, I would really appreciate you driving me on Tuesday," I say after a few moments pass. And if you want to stay while I get my cards read, I don't mind."

His smile grows and he leans over to press his lips to my cheek in a quick but sweet kiss.

His willingness to show public displays of affection in front of his teammates makes me feel extra special. I wasn't sure what his level of comfort would be there, but I'm happy he's comfortable with small acts. I don't need him to make out with me in public, but I am a touchy person and I like to hold hands like we're doing now. Thankfully, so far, that doesn't seem to bother him.

# CHAPTER EIGHTEEN

I TRIPLE CHECK that I have everything I need for our date tonight before finally putting the car in drive and heading over to Sasha's place.

I want tonight to be perfect, to show Sasha how much I actually like him, to prove to him that even though this is our first date and we are just starting out, I'm willing to put in the effort he deserves.

It's beyond evident to me that Sasha's ex did a real number on him by the way he reacts to the smallest of things. Like me offering to drive him to Karla's house on Tuesday. He acted like it was such a big deal when, in reality, it's nothing. I meant it when I told him I would drive him even if we weren't dating. That's what decent people do. They help you out when they can and don't expect anything in return. I know his friends act like this toward him, but clearly, he thinks things should be different now that we're dating. Which pisses me off to no end. I hope Sasha's ex is miserable in his life. Scumbags like him don't deserve happiness.

Rays of sunshine like Sasha, on the other hand, deserve all the happiness in the world.

When I pull up to the house where Sasha lives with a few of his friends, I take a deep breath before getting out of my car and walking up to the front door like a gentleman.

"Hey, Rio," Max, Sasha's roommate and, I guess, landlord

greets me. "Sasha will be down in a couple of minutes. He was having a wardrobe catastrophe, or at least that's what he claimed was going on."

I chuckle. "It's all good. I don't mind waiting."

"Is he here?" Sasha shrieks from upstairs.

"Take your time, babe. We've got plenty of time," I call up to him.

"You know that's still probably not going to calm his nerves, right?" Max states, and I shrug.

"It's the thought that counts, right?"

Max laughs and nods. "I'm glad Sasha's going out with you. You're a good guy."

"Thanks," I reply quietly. "He deserves to be treated like the gem that he is."

"I'm sorry for keeping you waiting," Sasha says, rushing down the stairs and nearly tripping at the bottom. Thankfully, I'm able to move quickly enough to catch him before his face hits the floor.

"Stop worrying about being late," I tell him as I hold his shaking body. "I'd much rather be hours late than see you get injured because you were rushing."

He takes a deep breath and then nods. "You're right. Please don't tell Hailey I almost fell. She's already been lecturing me on being careful because the team can't afford to have me out of commission."

I smile at him, then gently kiss his lips, not caring that Max is still here.

"She's right. You're our good luck charm. Now, the next time we go out, if you're running late, you know that it's okay, and I'm never going to be upset about running a little behind schedule."

He finally smiles at me, and the tension visible lifts off his shoulders. "You're too good for me," he whispers.

"It's the other way around, I assure you."

"Aww, you two are just the cutest," Max coos, and Sasha sticks his tongue out at him.

"We're leaving now," he tells his friend before dragging me out the door.

"Slow down," I remind him, pulling on his hand to slow him down. "We aren't in a rush tonight, and I haven't had a minute to take you in." I pause, then take a step back to get a good look at my date.

He has on a pair of dark wash jeans, an oversized gray sweater that looks comfortable and warm, just like I told him, and a pair of black sneakers. His hair is up in a messy bun that I can't wait to take out later tonight so I can run my fingers through his hair.

"You're breathtaking as always," I tell him once I've had my fill.

"And you're a flatterer as per usual," he mumbles with a smirk.

"You love it, don't lie," I reply, stepping closer once more and placing my hands on his hips.

"Okay, I won't lie," he tells me, and then I kiss him.

This time, it isn't a chaste kiss to get him out of his head. It's fiery and passionate, and I groan when we have to separate.

"As much as I'd love to stay here all night and make out, I do have something planned for us, and I'd hate for us to miss it," I tell him, grabbing his hand and pulling him to my car.

"Are you going to tell me what it is yet?" he asks, and I shake my head.

"Absolutely not. I told you it was a surprise, and I'm sticking to it."

He smiles, then gets into my car, and I rush around to get behind the wheel.

The drive to the park is fast, and Sasha sings along to the radio the entire time, showing off his amazing vocal talents.

"I love hearing you sing," I tell him as the song comes to an end, and I find a parking spot.

"I'm okay," he mumbles, clearly not believing just how talented he is.

"You're more than okay," I assure him. "How come you never pursued Broadway? You can dance and sing, and I have no doubt you'd be a fantastic actor as well."

"The original dream was to be a famous ballet dancer," he says while staring out the window. "I spent my entire childhood with that in mind, but life happened, and I had to give up that dream. After that I was just focusing on surviving. That's how I ended up in Green Spring. It was the exact opposite of everything I ever wanted in my life, but that also means it would be the last place he would ever look for me."

"Who?" I ask, and he shakes his head before plastering on a fake smile.

"It doesn't matter now. I'm sure he's long forgotten about me. But the reason I never pursued Broadway is because I was focused on another main stage. Sometimes it still sucks that I'll never see my name in shiny lights, but at least I found some amazing people who will always be there for me. And now I get to be the center of attention in a different way, and I'm loving it more than I ever would have thought."

I smile at him, then lean over the center console to give him a quick kiss. "And you're amazing at it, just like anything you do. Now come on we've got a concert to get to."

"A concert?" Sasha repeats with wide eyes.

He casts quick glances around the park, and I pop the trunk, getting out to grab the supplies I gathered earlier.

Sasha gasps behind me once he's out of the car. "You packed us a picnic?"

"I did. Along with extra blankets and a few pillows. A local band is putting on a concert in the park tonight. I hope that's okay with you."

He wraps his arms around me before I can grab the

supplies and nods his head against my chest. "It's more than okay. Thank you for thinking of such an awesome first date."

I hold him for a moment, then kiss the top of his head. "You don't have to thank me. That's what someone is supposed to do when they take you out on a date. This is where I'm supposed to be wooing you, so let me."

He chuckles, then lets me go, and I turn around to grab the supplies.

"Can I carry anything?" he checks, but I shake my head.

"I've got it all. Just follow me and help pick out the perfect spot," I tell him.

He does just that, picking a spot on the hill a bit farther away from the stage than most people are, probably to give us some privacy, which I don't mind at all.

"What did you pack in the picnic?" he asks as I set everything up.

"Unfortunately, it's nothing fancy," I apologize. "But it's edible, so that's a plus."

He laughs while we take a seat on the blanket. "I don't care about fancy, but I am grateful that it's edible," he teases.

I pull out premade sandwiches from a mom-and-pop shop I've always loved eating it along with a fruit and veggie platter. "There is a turkey club, a BLT sandwich, and a tomato something that I can't remember the name of," I tell him as I arrange everything.

"They look amazing," he whispers, licking his lips as he eyes the sandwiches.

"Which one would you like?" I check with him while pulling out a couple of paper plates.

"The BLT sounds delicious," he responds, so I place it on a plate for him and hand it over.

"How did you come up with this date idea?" he asks before taking a bite of his sandwich, moaning as he chews.

The noises cause my cock to stir, and I suck in a sudden

breath. I'm not used to having reactions like this, and they are going to take some getting used to.

It takes a moment before I feel like I can talk without sounding as turned on as I am, but eventually, I'm able to respond to his question. "I saw a post on social media when I was scrolling last night. I figured it would be perfect because it's low-key but still fun."

He nods and smiles as the band starts to play. We eat our meal in comfortable silence as we listen to the band play covers of well-known songs. People closer to the stage dance and sing along with the band. I enjoy taking in the scene around us, but my gaze always drifts back to the gorgeous man at my side.

"I think this is the best date I've ever been on," Sasha admits quietly after we've finished our food.

His head is resting on my shoulder and the band is now playing what they announced as an original. It's a ballad, and I find myself gently swaying to the beat.

"Does that mean you would be open to more dates?" I check.

He tilts his head toward me and there is a soft smile on his lips. "I would love nothing more than to go on a *lot* more dates with you."

I shift a little so I can lean into Sasha and steal a kiss that he immediately melts into. Since we are in public, I try not to get carried away, keeping the kiss gentle and PG-rated.

Eventually, we break for air and turn our attention back to the band. As we listen in comfortable silence, I pull him into my arms so that his back is resting against my chest. I've always enjoyed cuddling with those that I've built a deeper connection with, but I don't think anyone has felt as good in my arms as Sasha does right now.

"This has been one of the best nights of my life," Sasha whispers as the band starts to pack up and other people around us begin to leave.

"Mine too," I tell him honestly while still holding him tightly, not wanting to let him go just yet. "Would you like to come back to my place for a bit?"

Sasha turns in my arms with a giant grin and nods. "I'd love that."

The drive to my apartment is mostly quiet except for the low hum of the radio. The silence doesn't bother me, but it does give me the opportunity to get stuck in my head.

I know I'm the one who invited Sasha back to my place but what I don't know is what he's expecting to happen. Would he be happy with just cuddling and making out or would he want more? Am I ready for more? I'm not sure. I think I am, but I've thought that in the past and when I got into the bedroom with my partner, I couldn't get it up, even though I wanted to. I already feel a deeper sexual and emotional connection with Sasha than I have with others I've dated, but that doesn't do a lot to settle my insecurities.

I like Sasha and I want him, I really do, but sometimes what my brain wants and what my body wants can be two different things. I just really don't want to disappoint him if we get up to my room and he's expecting sex, but my cock isn't on board.

"Are you all right?" Sasha asks as I'm pulling into my parking lot. "Your hands are shaking."

I put the car into park before turning to him and taking a deep breath. "I'm nervous," I confess quietly.

He tilts his head to the side. "About what?"

"About what happens when we get to my room."

His eyes fill with understanding, and he reaches over to run his fingers gently over my cheek. "I don't have any expectations for tonight," he assures me. "We could spend the night playing video games on the couch with your roommates. Or we could spend our time in your room cuddling. *Or* we could do more if that's what you want, but I really don't care. I agreed to come back to your place because I didn't want this

**115**

night to end, but I don't care what we do as long as I get to spend more time with you."

His words push away my anxiety, and I feel like I can finally breathe again.

"Are you sure?" I check, and he chuckles.

"I'm *positive*. I know I've built a reputation for myself, and everyone sees me as the guy who is only wanting sex, but there's more to me than that. Sex isn't all I care about, especially not with you. We're building a relationship here, or at least I'd like to think we are." I nod so he knows I'm on the same page. "Then it's okay if we take things slow. We'll have all the time in the world to have sex when we're both ready, but that doesn't have to be tonight."

I smile at him and take a deep breath. "Thank you for being so understanding."

"Always," he assures me.

We both get out of my car, and I grab his hand to walk him to my apartment.

Monster and Bronny are playing a video game when we enter our place and they both look at us at the same time.

"I take it the date went well," Bronny questions with a waggle of his brows and smirk.

"It did, but it's not over," I tell them, keeping Sasha's hand in mine. "So, if you wouldn't mind, please leave us alone and only disturb us if there's an emergency."

Monster nods with a big grin, and Bronny whistles at us as we disappear into my room.

"Our friends are ridiculous," Sasha says with laughter in his tone as I close my door behind us.

"They are," I agree while kicking off my shoes and taking off my jacket. "Would you like to watch a movie or something?"

"Sure," he replies with a big grin before also removing his shoes and pulling his oversized sweater over his head, leaving him in a tight, long-sleeved shirt.

I grab the remote for my television before climbing into bed, propping myself up with pillows, and opening my arms as an invitation for Sasha to join me. He quickly gets into position, resting his back against my chest like he did when we were at the park.

"There's something I've been dying to know," Sasha says while I'm scrolling through the shows trying to find something we'll both like.

"What's that?" I question, but don't stop scrolling.

"I've been *dying* to hear the full story of how you got your nickname," he says, repositioning himself in my arms so his head is now resting in the crook of my elbow.

There's a shit eating grin on his face, and I can't help but laugh, finally stopping my scrolling. I was really hoping he'd forget all about that stupid story, but here we are.

"Is that so?" I check and he nods with that perfect smile of his.

"We got interrupted last night," he reminds me. "Which was totally unfair. So now that we have all the time in the world, you need to tell me."

"Do I now?" I question with a smirk of my own.

"Absolutely. First dates are usually about getting to know one another, what better way to do that than spilling the tea."

I chuckle. "Be prepared to be bored out of your mind," I warn him. "Like I said last night, it's not *actually* an exciting story."

Sasha rolls his eyes. "I don't care I still want to hear it."

"Fine," I sigh. "When I was fifteen, I was assigned a project to do a report on Rio. Keep in mind the main subject of that section was *life*. Everyone's assignment was different and there were a bunch of different categories. Some of those categories were books, movies, real life events, and locations. On the paper of my assignment, it said location, but I kind of skimmed over that."

Sasha's eyes go wide, and he covers his mouth as he waits for me to continue.

"So instead of doing my report on Rio de Janeiro, Brazil, and the people who live there, I wrote about the *movie* Rio and the impact it had on society."

Sasha snickers before waving his hand and apologizing.

"My soccer team thought it was hilarious and since Art was kind of a lame nickname, they started calling me Rio. It stuck, obviously, but I always felt like a dumbass when I told the story, so I just stopped and let people think what they wanted. There have been a bunch of different theories since I started here. I think my favorite is that I accidentally switched boarding passes with someone, and instead of going to my real location, I ended up in Rio. Which is a *way* better story than the truth."

"I don't know, the original is pretty decent," he tells me with a bright grin. "And I feel honored to know it when most people don't."

"If you tell anyone, I'll break up with you," I grumble which only has Sasha laughing.

"Your secret is safe with me, but wait. You said your old nickname was Art. What is your *real* name?"

I was expecting his question, and as stupid as it is, I don't mind telling Sasha the truth. "Arthur Henry Leon."

"That's a mouthful," he responds, and I nod. "My full name is Nathaniel Sasha Erikson. I used to go by Nate but changed it when I moved to Green Spring."

"Does that have something to do with your ex?" I ask.

"Yeah," he whispers, averting his eyes.

"How bad were things with him?" I inquire while running one of my hands up and down his side.

"Bad," he tells me while staring at my chest. "Really fucking bad."

I press a kiss to the top of his head and even though it's a faint sound, I don't miss his little sniffle. "I'm here when you're ready to tell me your story."

He finally looks back into my eye and offers me a small smile. "I appreciate that. I think it's just going to take some time. I've only ever told one person about what I went through and that was a therapist."

"There's no rush. Just know that I'm not going anywhere, and whatever you say won't make me see you any differently."

"Thank you," he whispers before moving up in my arms and pressing his lips to mine.

I'm pretty sure he's using the kiss to change the subject, but I won't hold that against him. Whatever happened with his ex was traumatic, and he needs time before he's ready to talk about it.

The kiss starts out sweet and innocent but quickly turns heated. Hands roam over bodies, and tingles of desire shoot through my veins. I'm pleasantly surprised to find my cock growing hard from the pressure of Sasha's hip.

Without breaking the kiss, I slowly move us so that Sasha is lying beside me. As I lick into his mouth, I grind against his leg, pulling the neediest of mewls from his plush lips.

"You're fucking intoxicating," I tell him when we take a break for air.

"Right back at you," he responds, staring into my eyes with a lust-filled gaze.

I smash my lips back to his, swallowing his moans and whimpers. My cock is now hard as a rock, and I'm hating the barrier of clothes we have between us.

I trace my fingers along the hem of the shirt. "What do you think about ditching these restricting clothes?" I question with a raised brow while I continue to run my finger back and forth across his lower abs.

"Are you sure?" he questions while nibbling on his lower lip.

I nod and push my erection into his hip again. "I want you and these clothes are only standing in our way."

"Well, you aren't wrong about that," he replies with a grin.

We both quickly get to work removing our clothes, leaving only our underwear on before we start making out again.

"Your body is so fucking perfect," I whisper against his lips as I reposition us so that I'm now on top of him.

I take his lower lip between my teeth and smirk as a needy moan ripples up his throat. I flick my tongue out to lick the area I just nibbled before moving to kiss his jaw, neck, collarbone, and chest. I pause my path down his body to suck on his right nipple, smiling when he bucks his hips into me. I make a mental note of how sensitive his nipples are before continuing down his body.

When I reach his lower abs, I pause and look at him while digging my fingers into the waistband of his briefs.

"Are you sure?" he asks. "We don't have to go farther than we've already gone if you don't want to."

It warms my heart that he's being so kind and understanding, refusing to push me farther than I'm ready. It suddenly dawns on me that we both have areas that need patience, which makes us kind of perfect for each other in a way. It also erases a lot of my doubts. If I can be content with waiting for Sasha to open up about his past, then I have to trust that he's also telling the truth and really doesn't care about my lack of experience.

"I want more," I tell him while trailing my nose along the outline of his penis, inhaling his musky scent. "I don't think I'm ready for anal, but I do know I want to taste you."

"Jesus!" he cries out when I mouth at his cock through his briefs.

"Can I?" I ask, pulling at his waistband once again.

Sasha quickly bobbles his head and lifts his hips again so I can shove them down. His cock thumps against his abs once it's finally free, and I lick my lips as I take in just how perfect he is. His creamy skin is blemish free with hardly any hair. While it's obvious he grooms I also think that a lot of his lack of hair is simply from genetics. Which is kind of the opposite of me. I'm a hairy guy who shaves every other day to stop my beard from growing in.

After I've spent a few moments soaking in how attractive my guy is, I lean down to finally take his thick and uncut cock into my mouth. I let my tongue dance under his foreskin, which has him panting and vibrating with desire. With a gentle hand, I pull his excess skin back and then suckle on the crown before taking him farther into my mouth, hallowing my cheeks as I go.

A hand slides into my hair, pulling gently on the short strands.

"Damn baby, that feels so good," he mutters with a shaky voice.

I flick my gaze up and hold eye contact with him as I bob up and down on his perfect dick savoring the salty taste that's coating my tongue.

When I get the courage to take him deeper, swallowing him down my throat, he throws his head back with a loud gasp.

"I'm not going to last," he tells me, but I don't stop.

I want his release. I want to make him feel so good he loses control. I want so much that I get lightheaded from the desire that's shooting through my veins.

With my free hand, I shove it down my underwear and start to jack myself off as I continue to give Sasha what I hope is an amazing blow job. Judging by his needy mewls and whimpers, I'd say I'm doing a pretty good job.

"Shit. Shit. Shit!" he shouts as his cock swells and his delicious load fills my mouth.

I pick up the pace of my fist as I swallow every last drop of Sasha's intoxicating cum, and it doesn't take long before

I'm also cascading over the edge of orgasmic bliss. My eyes literally roll into the back of my head as I come so hard I'm afraid I'm going to black out. The only thing stopping me from calling out so loud my roommates would definitely hear is the cock in my mouth that is muffling my moan.

When I let Sasha out of my mouth, I'm a panting mess, and my man is blissed out with a drunk looking grin on his stunning face.

"I haven't come that hard in maybe forever," he tells me, opening his arms for me to join him.

"Same," I respond, but instead of laying in his arms, I climb out of the bed. "I'll be right there," I assure him when he eyes me skeptically. "I just want to change out of my cum soaked underwear."

Sasha chuckles as I strip them off and grab a towel off the floor to give myself a quick wipe. "I guess that's fair. You did a really good job making sure I don't have a mess to worry about. Maybe next time, I can return the favor."

I bite my lip before shutting the light off and climbing back into bed with my man.

"If you think I'm going to turn down you blowing me, you'd be sorely mistaken, but it's also going to have to wait until next time because I'm spent," I tell him, pulling the blankets over us.

"That works for me. If I wake up before you, I could be your alarm clock," he says in his flirty voice.

"That sounds a hell of a lot better than a regular alarm clock," I tell him before leaning in for a kiss.

"I can taste myself on your tongue," he informs me. "It's fucking hot."

I smile against his lips before kissing him again and again. I could spend forever kissing this man and holding him in my arms.

When we eventually separate, Sasha rests his head on my

chest. "I haven't actually slept in the same bed as someone since Lux," he confesses softly.

"Did you want me to take you home?" I check, realizing we haven't actually had the conversation about him spending the night. I kind of just assumed, which is wrong of me.

He shakes his head, his hair tickling my chin. "No, I want to stay."

I smile and hold him tighter. "I'm glad to hear that because I want you to stay too. But heads up now, I'm kind of a whore for cuddling. It's one of my favorite things to do with someone I like. Sometimes, that's all I want to do."

Sasha lifts up so he can give me a quick peck on the lips before snuggling into my arms again. "If all we did was make out and cuddle most of the time, I would be one hundred percent on board with that."

The last bit of anxiety that was floating around in my body slowly flutters away, and a serene sense of calm wraps around me.

Maybe I've finally found my special someone.

# CHAPTER NINETEEN

*Sasha*

THE SAME GENTLE snoring that woke me a week ago fills my ears as I slowly blink my eyes open. But this time, instead of being on an uncomfortable couch, I'm wrapped in the arms of the best guy ever. I snuggle into him taking a deep inhale of his manly odor. Fuck, he smells so good that it has my cock going from a semi to full mast instantly.

Wanting to make good on my promise of being his alarm clock, I trail my fingers down his chest and through his thick happy trail to his massive cock. I'm a size queen, so I've been with my fair share of large guys, but I'm pretty sure Rio is the biggest cock I've ever seen in real life. When people say someone is hung like a horse, this is what they mean. Not only is he long, but he's thick too, the perfect combination. My mouth waters at the mere idea of having him in my mouth. And my cock twitches at the thought of hopefully one day having him deep inside of me, filling me more than I've ever been filled before. Stretching my ass so wide that the delicious sting will have my eyes rolling into the back of my head.

I have to press my lips together to fight back the needy whimper that wants to escape. I don't want Rio to wake up until he's in my mouth.

Slowly, I shimmy down his body, trying to move as smoothly as possible so I don't jostle my sleeping man. When

I'm finally at face level with his crotch, I smile at his half hard cock. It's going to be so fun to have him growing inside my mouth until my lips are stretched so wide they almost hurt. I'm a pro at giving blow jobs, but I know taking Rio all the way down my throat isn't going to be easy. Thankfully, I'm really good at challenges and will try my hardest to take him as far as I can.

Quickly, I lick my lips before leaning in and trailing my tongue up his slowly growing erection. When I get to the tip, I swirl my tongue around him before sucking him into my mouth.

The snoring has stopped, and Rio's breathing has turned from slow and deep to shallow and quick. I hallow my cheeks while diving down more and smile when my man groans.

"Yes," he murmurs as I grip the base of his cock to give me a helping hand as he continues to grow. "Fuck, Sash, that's so good."

I don't think my name has ever sounded so good on someone's lips before.

"Your cock is so big," I tell him, coming up for air. "I can't wait until the day that you're ready to fuck me. It's going to feel so good being stretched that wide." I slide my hand up and down his cock as I talk dirty to him, loving the way he pulses in my grip. "You'd like that, wouldn't you? My tight hole choking your cock as you pound into me."

"Shiiiitttt," Rio groans out.

"Unless you're not a top," I inquire, realizing we haven't exactly had this conversation. "I've only topped once, but I'd be willing to try again."

He shakes his head, moaning when I tighten my grip on his dick. It's so big I'm unable to wrap my hand all the way around it.

"I-I-I'm a top," he stutters out, and I can't help but wiggle a little at his response.

"Perfect," I tell him before diving back down for another taste.

My jaw aches as I take him in, trying to relax my throat enough to swallow him down. I get pretty far, but I'm wondering if it might be impossible to take all of him into my mouth. Just because I can't swallow him down my throat doesn't mean I still can't give him the best blow job of his life. I have other tricks up my sleeve besides a talented throat.

I position myself so that I'm straddling his lower legs, then spit into both my palms before gripping his thick base. With my hands around him, I lower my mouth back to the head of his cock and begin bobbing up and down, using my hands to make up for the space I couldn't cover.

Rio's moans grow louder, and I'm pretty sure if his room-mates are awake right now, they'll be able to hear him. I couldn't care less if they hear because I love a noisy lover. It lets me know that I'm doing a good job. Getting my partner off is a massive turn on for me. Don't get me wrong, I *love* receiving pleasure, but there's something about giving and making someone come undone that gives me this heady feeling.

My own cock is throbbing between my legs, and I start to rub it against Rio's legs. The friction causes me to moan and hum, which must feel amazing to my sexy soccer player because he bucks into my mouth. I love it when a man loses control and lets his inner beast out. Maybe one day I could get Rio to really let loose and fuck my face.

"Jesus," Rio calls out when I purposefully hum around his cock for a second time.

When his hands move to my head and thread through my hair, my body ignites, and I pick up my speed, all the while humping his legs.

"Shit. Fuck. I'm close," he warns me a short while later.

I look into his eyes and nod at him, silently telling him to give it to me. It's like he was waiting for my permission because his head falls back, and he roars as hot ropes of salty cum shoot into my mouth. His load is so big that a bit of cum dribbles down my chin as I try to swallow as much as I can. He tastes like heaven and sin mixed together, and if it was possible to survive off of cum alone, I wouldn't want to put anything else in my mouth.

After Rio's orgasm is over, I let him out of my mouth and rise up on my knees, grabbing my cock and jerking off at a rapid speed. It doesn't take long before I reach my own release, and I'm covering his cock and abs with my seed. Damn, he looks hot, covered in my load.

"How is it I've managed to be the only one who gets dirty both times we've messed around now?" Rio asks after a moment, and I can't help but laugh.

"I'd be more than happy to get dirty with you," I tell him with a wink before climbing out of his bed to grab the towel he used to clean himself last night. It's a little crusty but it will do the job until he can get into a shower to really give himself a clean.

"You've got a really talented mouth," Rio says once I've climbed back under the covers with him.

"I wish I could have shown you how talented I really am, but you're so big I couldn't get my throat to relax enough," I tell him. "But practice makes perfect, so I'll just have to keep trying."

He laughs and runs his hand up and down my spine.

Being in Rio's arms like this is fucking perfect. Everything feels so easy and comfortable like this is exactly where I'm supposed to be. This is probably how a relationship is supposed to feel. Not forced and anxiety filled like things were with Lux.

I'm grateful Rio ended up in my life because I don't think I would have ever tried dating again without someone like him. He's fixing the broken things inside of me and teaching my brain how a real man treats their partner.

# CHAPTER TWENTY

SASHA and I walk hand in hand up the path to BooBoo's parents' house, and I don't know if I've ever been as happy as I am right now.

We've been officially dating for four days now but somehow it feels like longer. Maybe it's because we've known each other for a while now and have grown our friendship over the years. I've heard some demisexual people describe waking up one day and realizing that they like someone who has been in their life for a long time in a completely different way. It's like a sudden realization of feelings, and that pretty much nails my feelings for Sasha on the head. It went from friendship to interest to more so quickly that it caught me off guard. I'm just lucky that he feels the same way because that isn't always how it works.

"Hi Rio, it's nice to see you again," Karla greets me with a warm grin. "And you must be Sasha," she says, reaching out to grab his hand in both of hers.

"That's me," Sasha says with his usual flair. "And you're Karla?"

Her smile grows wider, and she nods. "Come on, I've got my room all set up. Are you joining us?" she checks with me, but I look at Sasha instead of responding.

"Yes, he is," he tells her, giving my hand a squeeze.

"Works for me," she says while leading us to her witchy room, as BooBoo calls it.

"This place is gorgeous," Sasha whispers with an awe-filled tone.

"Thank you, why don't you pick a deck, and I'll light some incense."

Sasha nods. He walks over to the table and instantly picks the same deck I did.

"This one was almost screaming at me," he says, and Karla shoots me a knowing smile.

"Should I grab another chair?" she asks, but Sasha shakes his head.

"I'll sit in Rio's lap. The chair looks sturdy enough to hold us both."

I sit first then Sasha perches in my lap and takes a deep inhale of the incense that Karla lit.

Karla pulls out the cards like she did for me and starts to shuffle them. "What are you wanting from today's reading?" she asks Sasha.

"I guess just a general reading," he says with a shrug. "It's been forever since I've had one, but when BooBoo and Rio mentioned you there was like this intense pressure inside of me that was telling me I had to come here. It left me wondering if my spirit guides have a message for me."

She nods, just like when I was here, cards begin to fly out of the deck, and she stops when there are five on the table.

She flips the first card and smiles when *The Lovers* card shows up. "That makes a lot of sense," she says, and I give Sasha a little squeeze. "As you know, the lovers in this upright position represent love, relationships, union, and harmony. Something I can see you clearly have in your life right now."

Sasha flashes me a smile and nods at Karla. A second card is flipped; this one is also upright. It shows people emerging from what looks like graves, extending their arms, and looking up at an angel blowing a trumpet in the sky. At the bottom of the card, Judgment is written, and Sasha hums, still smiling.

"The judgment card in this upright position signifies you are on the right path," she tells us, but I'm pretty sure Sasha already knows that.

The third card that she flips has my man gasping. This one is apparently called *The Tower*. The image on the card shows a tower that kind of looks like it's on fire and with people falling out of it.

"Just wait," Karla tells Sasha, who is shaking in my arms.

"What does the card mean?" I question, feeling out of the loop.

"Usually nothing good," Sasha mumbles. "It represents chaos, upheaval, and sudden change."

Shit that doesn't sound good at all. What kind of chaos could be lurking around the corner for him? A knot forms in my stomach but I force myself to be patient and hope that Karla has a better explanation once she's done.

The fourth card she flips is the *Wheel of Fortune, which, if I remember from my reading,* means change.

"As you know, this card represents change, but it also represents good luck and destiny," Karla tells me.

The final card she flips is called *The Star*. It has a naked woman in front of a lake pouring pitchers of water. There is a large yellow star at the top of the card and smaller white stars alongside it.

"*The Star* represents hope, healing, and renewal," Karla says and Sasha nods along. "To me, this reading is telling you that you are loved and on the exact path you are supposed to be, but trials will be coming your way. Something big is coming your way, and you need to be prepared. But good luck, hope, and healing will soon follow whatever chaos is thrown at you. You need to stay strong in your faith, in yourself, and those around you. Challenges are coming, but they won't last long, and good things are waiting for you on the other side."

"I've really had enough of the universe throwing shit at me," Sasha grumbles, and I run my hands up and down his arms.

"I understand that feeling all too well," Karla tells Sasha. "Even though we just met, I know you are strong. Your aura is one of the brightest ones I have ever seen. You are going to get through this."

Sasha sighs but nods. "Thank you. I really appreciate you taking time out of your day to do this reading for me."

Karla smiles warmly at my man. "Anytime. Please don't let *The Tower* card scare you too much. Put your focus more on the ones of positivity."

"I will," he responds, standing and rounding the table to give Karla a hug.

"I want you to take this deck and use it whenever you are feeling anxious," she tells Sasha who shakes his head.

"I couldn't do that. It looks so old and well loved," he replies.

"It is. It was a gift to me, and I'm gifting it to you. One day, in the future, you can pass it along to someone else."

Sasha gives Karla another hug, this one much tighter than the first. "Thank you," he whispers before letting her go.

She smiles and hands him the tarot deck.

"You are more than welcome."

Karla walks us to the door and reminds us not to be strangers.

On the drive back to Sasha's house, I can tell he's worried, but I don't know what to do to make it better.

"No matter what happens you have me and amazing friends surrounding you. You're going to be fine, just like Karla said," I remind him as I park outside his house.

He doesn't respond right away, but he nods to acknowledge my words.

"Deep down I know I'm going to be okay at the end, but my gut is also telling me that whatever is coming my way is going to completely turn my world upside down. I'm scared." His words are broken, and I see a tear trickle down his face. "How strong do I really have to be? Why does the universe keep testing me like this? I just want my happily ever after already and to be done with fear and sadness."

I reach over and grab his hand. "I'm sorry for everything you've ever gone through, and I'm even more sorry that you had to go through most of that alone, but you're not alone anymore," I remind him. "I won't ever abandon you, no matter what happens. Even if you decide that this relationship isn't meant to be, I will still be your friend. I care about you, and so do many other people. Please don't shut us out."

Sasha takes a shaky breath and nods. "I won't. Thank you for being so understanding."

"That's what partners do," I tell him with a wink.

He finally smiles and gives me a gentle shove before leaning in for a kiss and then heading into his house.

I hate that he's going to have to face more struggles, but I know that I'm going to be by his side the entire time.

# CHAPTER TWENTY-ONE

THIS MORNING, I drew a tarot card to help guide my day. It was the Justice card, which told me I needed to tell Rio about my past. The card is about being good and truthful, and while I haven't exactly lied to him, he deserves to know about my past to understand why I am the way I am. It's not going to be easy, but it has to happen.

I'm finishing up cleaning my room, making sure it's in decent shape when there is a knock at the front. I quickly rush down the stairs, knowing it's going to be Rio, and smile when I open the door.

"Hey, handsome," I greet him while stepping to the side to let him in.

"Hey yourself," he replies then kisses me as soon as I've shut the door.

"Ready for the movie marathon?" I ask, and he nods.

When I was inviting Rio over, I didn't want to say *hey we need to talk,* since no one wants to hear those words, so I came up with the idea of a movie marathon night. And at least if I chicken out on telling him my story, we'll still have something to do.

"I still can't believe you haven't seen any of the Final Destination movies," he says while shaking his head and following me up the stairs to my room.

"I told you I don't love gore," I mumble.

"They aren't really *that* gory, but you'll definitely get lots of good jump scares," he assures me.

I shut the door behind him, then sit on the bed and wait for Rio to join me.

"Before we start, I kind of want to tell you something," I say while fiddling with my fingers.

"What's up?" he asks and tilts his head.

"I think it's time that I tell you about my ex," I tell him, and his brows shoot up before he schools his expression.

"Are you sure?" he questions, and I nod.

"I pulled a tarot card this morning and I'm pretty sure that's what it was telling me to do. I know we've only been dating for about a week, but I really like you, and I think we have the possibility of a real future together. But the only way to make sure we start this off on the right foot is by me telling you about what I went through."

He grabs my hand and brings the knuckles to his lips to kiss gently. "I appreciate you wanting to tell me. If you believe you're ready, I'm here to listen."

I close my eyes and take a deep breath before telling the story I wish never happened.

"My mom passed away when I was fifteen, and I had to move in with a friend of hers. The lady was nice enough, and I knew her pretty well, but she wasn't my mom. We didn't talk a lot, mostly because she was trying to give me space. She didn't know how to deal with a grieving teenager, and I did my best to push her out of my life."

I take another deep breath because that wasn't even the hard part of my teenage years.

"Thankfully, my mother left me a decent amount of money in her will, and we were able to access some of those funds to cover things like my ballet fees, so I didn't lose another thing I loved. I put my all into dance and pushed my mom's friend even farther away. She tried her best, but I wanted nothing to do with her, and since she didn't know what to do, she let me have as much space as I wanted. When I was sixteen, the ballet studio I attended hired an eighteen-year-old instructor in training. His job was to shadow the main instructor and learn the ins and outs of being an instructor. He also worked one-on-one with a few of the students who needed or wanted extra help. I was one of those students."

My hands shake as the memories start coming back.

"At first, Lux was very professional, but he could tell I had a crush on him and used that to his advantage. He became my friend and got me to tell him everything about my life. When he asked me out six months after meeting, I thought I was the luckiest boy alive. Of course, we had to keep it a secret since the studio wouldn't have looked fondly on our relationship, but I didn't care because I was already head over heels for him. Since I really didn't have anyone in my life it was easy for him to become my everything. He hooked me in so easily, and I fell for every single one of his lies. He convinced me to change who I was so that I would be able to get a job at the New York City Ballet once I was old enough. But in reality, it was just because those were his personal preferences. He took control of every aspect of my life, and I became just a shell of myself."

I pause again, taking a shaky breath. Damn, this is hard to get out.

"By the time I turned seventeen Lux had me lying to my mom's friend so much I almost started believing the lies myself. I would tell her that I needed money for dance things or school when in reality, it was just to give to Lux. I don't even remember anymore how much money I gave him that he blew on only God knows what. But I thought I loved him, so I just kept giving him more and more money.

Eventually I moved in with him even though my mom's friend tried to stop me. I just screamed at her that she wasn't my mother and never would be. She eventually let me go, but

I could tell the decision was hard for her. She knew that Lux wasn't a good man, and I should have listened to her."

Tears bubble in my eyes as I remember all the hurtful things I said to Anna because I was young and stupid.

"Things went from bad to worse, but I had no way out, at least, that's what I thought. I was crying myself to sleep every night, praying for a way out that seemed impossible. The emotional and verbal abuse started pretty early on. He loved to tell me how stupid I was and point out all my flaws. He thrived on making me feel small, and he was so good at it. It wasn't until after I was living with him that the physical abuse started." Rio rubs my shoulder but doesn't say anything, allowing me to continue.

"He warned me time and time again that if I left him, he would hunt me down and kill me, and I believed him, so I stayed. I stayed until one day he beat the shit out of me so badly that I'm still surprised I'm alive." Rio gasps this time, and I take a shaky breath before continuing. "As I was lying in the hospital bed with a wired shut jaw, I figured if I was going to die anyway, I might as well take the risk and run away. And I could do it while Lux was in jail. Although I knew he wouldn't be in there for long, so I had to act fast. I spent hours looking online for a place where he would never look for me, and I stumbled upon Green Spring, Michigan. As soon as I was discharged from the hospital, I booked a plane ticket and left on the next available flight. But before I left, I sent an email to the ballet studio where I danced and told them everything that happened. I have no idea how he took that or what happened, but I can't imagine he was pleased about it.

Not only was he losing me, his cash cow, but also probably his job. But I couldn't find it in me to care anymore. When I left, I only took what I could fit in a backpack because I didn't have time to pack more. Thankfully, I was already eighteen when this happened, so I had a credit card and was able to make all the bookings myself. I spent my first few months here looking over my shoulder, but eventually, I realized he wasn't coming and that this was the fresh start I needed. The homeless shelter I was staying at gave information about the college and was able to help me sign up for classes. The only smart thing I did when I was with Lux was not tell him exactly how much money my mom had left me.

Thankfully, I still had enough to pay for my first few years of college, and after that, I got student loans. That's why I have to keep working because I didn't have a free ride, but it was a start, and without that money I doubt I would have gotten my life in order like I did. I kick myself in the ass every day for Lux's lies and believing that he loved me, but I also thank my lucky stars just as much that I was able to get out alive."

Rio pulls me into his arms, holding me tightly and rocking me. "Fuck, baby, I'm sorry you had to go through that."

I sniffle back a tear and nod into his shoulder. "It's why I always question the nice things you do for me because Lux wasn't like that. And if he ever did do something nice and caring, it was for a strategic reason."

"Thank you for telling me all of this. I can understand your hesitations more now," he whispers, continuing to rock me. "Your ex was a grade-A asshole who took advantage of you and should be in jail for the shit he did to you. But I'll never stop thanking the universe enough that you got out alive and were able to show up in my life."

"I don't deserve a man as sweet as you," I tell him, but he shakes his head.

"You deserve this and so much more. If your mom was still here, I know she would tell you that. And I'll spend every day until I can't talk anymore, reminding you of it as well. You are an amazing person, Sasha, and I'm in awe of you. I'm the lucky one in this relationship."

I take a shaky breath and wipe away the few tears that

managed to break free. "Okay, it's time to cuddle and watch those ridiculous movies," I say, grabbing my tablet off my nightstand.

"I'm so on board with that plan," he tells me and kisses my cheek.

I really hope that whatever the universe is going to throw at me doesn't take Rio away from me.

# CHAPTER TWENTY-TWO

THE CROWD ROARS as we celebrate another win, and I can't help but grin like a fucking fool as Sasha jumps around the field in his Kerrington costume.

I was beyond pissed after he told me about what his asshole of an ex did to him, but I was also extremely happy that he found the strength to tell me. It gives me a better understanding of things to do and things to avoid when it comes to my man, who is quickly becoming my world. That might be insane to some since we've only been dating for a little over a week. But we've been friends for a lot longer, so I think that's the difference. We already had an emotional bond and are just now moving to a different space.

After our celebration on the turf, I follow my teammates to the locker room for our post-game chat with Coach and a quick shower.

After all of that is finished, I make my way to the mascot changing room and knock on the door.

"How are you always faster than me?" Sasha asks with wet hair and a tiny pout. He's wearing a large GSU sweater that matches mine, and I can't help but smile at how cute we look together.

"Because I don't stand around chatting for forever," I tease him, and he rolls his eyes, but his smile grows all the same. "Are you ready to go?"

"Yup. Tricia told me she'd swing by and grab the Kerrington costume in the morning, so I don't even have to transport it anywhere," he tells me with a goofy grin while mentioning one of the other mascot members.

"Perfect, that means I can actually rest after the game," I joke.

Sasha gives me a playful shove while scoffing. "You don't ever *have* to carry my costume after the games."

"I know," I say, wrapping my arm around his shoulder while we make our way to the parking lot. "But I also like doing that kind of stuff for you," I remind him.

He smiles at me so brightly it makes my heart beat a little faster. Sasha is perfect for me, and sometimes I want to kick myself for not seeing it sooner. For not allowing him to get closer sooner. Maybe if I hadn't written him off as an annoying flirt and saw who he really was in our first year of knowing each other, I might have noticed my other feelings for him sooner. But playing the game of 'what ifs' is pointless because we can't change the past. The only thing I can do is cherish my time with him now and continue to build a future with him.

"Do your teammates know how much of a softie you are?" he asks me.

I narrow my eyes at him, but the grin that has almost become a permanent part of my face remains. "If you tell anyone about my sweet side, I'll have to kill you."

Sasha throws his head back, laughing, and it fills me with a warmth I've never experienced before. I can't put my finger on what the feeling means. Is it love? No. It can't possibly be. It's far too soon, isn't it? I mean, I've never been in love before, so I don't know exactly what that feels like. At this point in time, I don't think it matters what exactly this feeling means. I'm sure I'll figure it out eventually. Until then, I'll just revel in how good it feels.

"Rio!" someone shouts as we enter the parking lot.

Some of my teammates are standing around a woman with bright red curly hair who's holding her phone out and looks like she's interviewing them. Behind her is a guy with a camera who might also be recording what's going on or taking pictures, which isn't unusual since there are quite a few college blogs and such. BooBoo is amongst the guys and waves me over, so I guide Sasha in their direction.

"What's up?" I question them once we're close enough that I don't have to shout.

"Lyla here is interviewing us about our games so far this season," BooBoo tells me.

"I'm currently live on our GSU sports page," she tells me, pointing her phone in my direction. "Mind if I ask you a few questions?"

I shrug while keeping my arm around Sasha's shoulder. His eyes meet mine, and he subtly tilts his head to the side, silently asking if he should step out of the frame, but I don't let him go. I'm not ashamed of him, and I don't care if the whole world knows we're dating. But I do pay attention to his body language to make sure he's okay with being here because I don't want to pressure him into staying. When he melts into my side and beams at me, I know we're on the same page.

Lyla begins asking questions about the team and brings up stats about me that I'm impressed she's memorized. I answer the questions easily, loving to have the chance to talk about the sport I love so much.

We're on our third or fourth question when a bunch of whistling, cheering, and catcalling happens, and I turn around to find a few of my teammates mooning the camera. BooBoo is in the middle shaking his ass like he's at a club which has both me and Sasha doubling over in laughter.

"Fuck," Lyla cusses, and I turn back around to find a very angry redhead.

Does this woman not have a sense of humor at all? I mean, yeah it disturbed the interview, but it *is* funny.

"Are you okay?" I ask her, and she damn near growls.

Sasha and I take a step back at the exact same time and share a look that says, "*what the fuck is going on?*"

"Your teammates just got our lives banned. Not only was this broadcast shutdown, but we probably won't be able to go live again for who knows how long."

Shit. I didn't think about that. I guess I see why she's angry now.

"Sorry," I apologize on behalf of my teammates, but that doesn't seem to appease her.

She huffs out a breath and rolls her eyes. "Whatever." With those parting words, she turns on her heels and stomps away.

"Don't worry about her," the guy who was also recording says. "She might be pissed that we can't go live for a while, but her attitude will change when we go viral, thanks to your friends there." He waves at us before following his friend, coworker, or whatever they are to each other.

"You guys pissed off Lyla," I shout out at the guys who shrug.

"She just needs a sense of humor," BooBoo shouts back.

"Ready for me to take you home?" I check with Sasha who's still snickering.

"I guess so," he says once he's composed himself. "I wish I didn't have classes first thing in the morning so we could spend more time together tonight."

"A couple of evenings apart isn't going to kill us," I remind him as we make our way to my car, but a pang of disappointment flutters in my chest. I'd like to spend as much time together with Sasha as possible. "It's not like we're going weeks without seeing each other."

He sighs and pouts. "I know, but I'm already becoming addicted to your cuddles."

I laugh, then kiss his cheek. "I am a fantastic cuddler," I reply in a cheeky tone.

He rolls his eyes, but his lips slowly turn up at the sides. He loves my teasing, even if he won't ever admit it out loud. And I love the way he gives it right back. That's what makes us so good for each other.

# CHAPTER TWENTY-THREE

SWEAT DRIPS down my back as I move to the music, smiling at Carter as he dances almost like a pro. When the music stops, I grab a towel I left on the floor and wipe the sweat off my forehead.

"I don't think you need me anymore," I tell Carter, who is downing his water.

"You're not firing me as a client, are you?" he questions, and I shake my head.

"Nah, I'll continue to take your money and dance with you for as long as you want, but you really don't need the classes anymore."

He shrugs. "Maybe not, but I like having this as part of my routine."

I smile at him and nod. I love spending time with Carter, and even though I get to show off on the sidelines now, dancing in a setting like this is still different. I'm grateful that we were able to find a space at the school to continue our lessons. Even though Carter definitely doesn't need me anymore, I think I would feel lost if I couldn't practice my ballet from time to time.

"Well, I'm glad you are willing to pay to spend time with me," I tease, then pause. "Wait, does that make me like a friend hooker?"

Carter laughs while shaking his head. "Nah. You're a real

friend who still teaches me something new every time we get together and deserves to be compensated for his expertise."

I chuckle and wave my off. "Well, I appreciate it. And since you're so eager to keep learning, I'm excited to work on your Fouetté next week."

He throws his head back with a groan at the mention of one of the most difficult turns in ballet. "Fuck, maybe I should fire you."

I laugh as we pack up our bags. "I'd maybe believe you if you didn't just confess to loving me so much," I tease with a wink.

My phone beeps in my bag, and I pull it out, shaking my head. I see another video using the clip from Sunday's interview.

Carter glances over my shoulder and chuckles. "You guys are internet famous," he says, and I roll my eyes.

"It's the asses in the background that people really want to see. I'm just there out of sheer coincidence."

The guys are lucky they didn't get in more shit with the university about the stunt they pulled. The only repercussion they are facing is having to sit out one game. It's going to suck, but it could have been far worse.

"Should I get your autograph now before you get *really* famous?" he jokes, and I give him a playful shove.

Ever since Rio's idiot teammates decided to moon that reporter on Sunday, my face has been everywhere. I was a little anxious when the video started blowing up like it did since I've done everything in my power to stay under the radar since I moved to Green Spring. But I've been able to push most of that anxiety to the side. I mean, it's been seven years since I left Lux; there's no way he could still be looking for me, right?

We bullshit as we head down the hall, and I wave at him when I need to take my exit and then make the short walk to my house.

An eerie shudder creeps up my spine as I walk along the sidewalk, and I keep looking over my shoulder, but I never see anyone out of the ordinary. I really hate how much of a hold Lux still has on me, even after all this time. It's highly unlikely that he's going to hunt me down after all this time, but my subconscious hasn't gotten that memo and is still on high alert for no reason.

When I get home, I shut the door behind me and sigh.

"Are you all right?" Max asks, and I shake my head.

"That stupid video going viral is stirring up feelings from my past, and now I can't even walk down the street without thinking someone is following me," I tell him as my heart races.

"Shit, come sit down," he instructs, rushing over to grab my hand and guide me to the couch. "You think someone was following you?" he checks.

I shake my head. "Not really. I didn't see anyone, but I couldn't shake this creepy feeling either. I'm pretty sure it's just my mind playing tricks on me. When I left California, I ran away from a really bad guy who told me if I ever left him, he'd hunt me down and kill me. I doubt he's still looking for me, but I'm still scared nonetheless."

"Shit," Max mutters while wrapping an arm around my shoulder. "I'm sorry that you're going through this right now. Is there anything I can do to help?"

I shrug. "Unless you can rewire my brain, I don't think anything is going to help."

"I could drive you to classes when I'm not working," he offers, and as much as I don't want to accept help, it's not a bad idea.

"I'd really appreciate that," I tell him with a smile. "I could probably also ask Rio to drive me around when you can't. At least then I won't have to worry about being alone. Like I just said, I'm sure I'm overreacting, but if using the buddy system will stop my panic attacks, I'm all for it."

"We've got you. You have good people in your life now, and we won't let you down."

I smile at him before taking a deep breath as the panic slowly lifts off my shoulders.

I'm not alone. And I'll never be alone again.

# CHAPTER TWENTY-FOUR

WATCHING Sasha look over his shoulder constantly the past few days has my heart breaking for him. When he asked me if I would be okay with driving him around for a little while I said yes without hesitation. He claims that deep down he knows Lux won't come looking for him but being around others calms his anxiety. I would do anything to help the man who is already claiming a permanent place in my heart.

We've been dating for two weeks today, but it feels like months. We've fallen into an easy routine, and he's pretty much all I can think about when I'm not with him—well, him and soccer. Dating Sasha comes so naturally that it has me wondering if soul mates are a real thing. I've never felt so content in all of my life, and it's simply because I have this amazing man as my partner. He just makes everything a little bit better.

Everyone around me has noticed the subtle change, even Coach, who simply slapped me on the shoulder and told me happiness looks good on me.

"Are you excited to get away for a little bit?" I ask Sasha as the bus drives us for another away game.

He nods with a big smile. "I'm beyond excited. I already feel like I can breathe a little deeper. If Lux *was* looking for me, which he probably isn't, but *if* he was, he wouldn't have any idea that I'd be traveling with the soccer team. Only you guys and those in charge know that I'm the mascot."

I give his hand a squeeze and press my lips to his cheek. Fuck I hate that he is harboring so much anxiety about that stupid video going viral. I really wish I had connections to figure out what happened to that Lux guy so I could give Sasha peace of mind. I don't think this fear is going to go away until he knows that Lux isn't a threat. It took him half a year to stop worrying when he first moved here, and that was when Lux had no way of finding him. Heaven only knows how long it's going to take to calm his nerves this time. Although the last time Sasha was all alone, and now, he has a massive support system so maybe it won't be so bad.

In the meantime, all I can do is continue to be part of Sasha's support system, which I will do for as long as he is in my life.

THE ENERGY on the bus is electric after *another* fantastic win. Sasha really is our good luck charm.

"Three cheers for Kerrington," BooBoo shouts as we make our way to the hotel. "Hip-Hip."

"Hooray!" everyone cheers, causing Sasha to turn the brightest shade of pink.

"Hip-Hip," BooBoo calls out again.

"Hooray!" the team yells back louder.

"Hip-Hip," BooBoo says one last time, and the final hooray that follows is loud you can practically feel the words vibrating through your chest.

"You all might think I'm your good luck charm," Sasha says while kneeling on his chair so everyone can see him. "But your talent is the real reason you're bringing home those wins. Although I won't complain about getting to tag along for this amazing journey."

Everyone hoots and hollers in agreement when Sasha sits back down, and I lean over to steal a quick kiss.

"I'm really glad you're along for the journey," I whisper to him, making him blush even harder.

"I don't think I've ever blushed this much in my life," he tells me with a toothy grin.

"You just need to figure out how to take a compliment better. You're amazing, and everyone can see it. That's why we love having you at every game. Well, that and our stupid superstitions."

He chuckles and nods. "This team is amazing, so it's really no hardship at all to be with you guys for every game."

"BooBoo said if you wanted to sneak into our room tonight to cuddle that he wouldn't care. We're just not allowed to fuck," I tell him, and his eyes light up.

"Really?" he asks, and I nod. "Well, I'm not going to turn that down. You already know what an amazing cuddler you are. I'll let Hailey know so she can cover for me in case someone does room checks."

Sasha is practically vibrating with excitement as we pull up to the hotel.

"I'm going to clear things with Hailey. Text me once you have your room number, and I'll meet you there," he tells me as we get off the bus. Then he pecks my cheek and rushes off to find his friend.

"You still good with the plan?" I check with BooBoo as we wait for our room assignments and key cards.

He nods. "But I meant what I said. If you two start fucking, I'm going to pour ice water on you."

I laugh and hold my hands up. "No need to threaten such levels of violence."

It doesn't take long for us to get our key cards, and BooBoo and I head to our room to get settled.

"Are you hanging out with Hailey until curfew?" I check, and he shrugs.

"She said she had to call her grandpa. I guess it's his birthday, and now is the best time to get ahold of him. If she gets off before then, we might hang out."

"You guys sure seemed to be getting cozy on the bus," I note, making him blush.

"She's pretty awesome."

"Why haven't you asked her out yet?" I inquire.

"Because I'm pretty sure she'll shoot me down, and I haven't always been the best at handling rejection. I mean, I don't pull any bro shit and get mad at the girl, but I always end up feeling really down afterward. Especially when it's someone I'm *really* into, like Hailey."

I nod. "I get it. Being demi means I'm not sexually attracted to someone until I've developed a close relationship with them. And sometimes, when those feelings do show up, the other person has no interest in you that way at all, and it can sting like a bitch."

A knock on the door stops our conversation, and I instantly move to open it.

"Long time no see," Sasha says when I open the door.

"I know it's been *ages*," I joke back.

"Are you sure you're cool with this?" he asks BooBoo, who nods.

"Absolutely, I still feel bad about that video going viral, so consider this my apology."

BooBoo doesn't know all the details about why Sasha has been on edge, but after a mini panic attack this morning when BooBoo tried to scare Sasha, I had to fill him in on the basics.

"It's not your fault. Nobody knows that I was hiding from someone. And it has been seven years, so in theory, that person shouldn't be a threat anymore."

"It still sucks that you had to be put in the spotlight without your permission," BooBoo mumbles.

"Shit happens," Sasha tells him with a shrug. "I promise I'm not mad at anyone. And I'm sure my anxiety will go down in the next couple of weeks once the smoke settles and we aren't as viral as we are now."

BooBoo nods, but having known him for as long as I have, I can tell he's still beating himself up, which I completely understand. I've also spent some time beating myself up over being the reason Sasha was in that video in the first place. But no one could have predicted how viral that video got, so there really isn't anyone to blame.

"Should we check out the TV guide and see if there's anything good on?" Sasha suggests, and both BooBoo and I nod.

Sasha grabs the remote then we both get comfortable on our bed while BooBoo settles in on his.

There's a channel playing back-to-back reruns of the office, so we turn it on and spend some time vegging and laughing as we relax.

A good laugh session is exactly what all of us needed.

# CHAPTER TWENTY-FIVE

THE ENTIRE WEEK FLEW BY, and before I know it, I'm back in the mascot costume cheering on the GSU soccer team. Since this is a home game, I have a few more of the cheer squad with me tonight and am able to perform more than I am at away games, which is always a great time. Although I have stumbled a few times tonight when I look too closely at the crowd. I keep imagining that Lux is there even though I know he isn't. Thankfully, no one has mentioned my mishaps.

This game has been a lot closer than the other ones since their major loss and I'm pretty sure the entire crowd is biting their nails hoping the team pulls off another win.

"What is up with them tonight?" Rebecca whispers.

"I might actually have something to do with that," Hailey replies, sounding nervous.

"What the hell did you do?" Rebecca whisper shouts.

"Nothing," Hailey responds, holding her hands up. "BooBoo asked me out before the game, and I told him I needed time to think about it."

"Shit," I say, making sure to keep my voice low so no one hears me.

"What do you need to think about?" Rebecca asks. "He's hot, and you talk about him all the time. Just go over there and tell him yes already."

Hailey bites her nail while staring at BooBoo on the field, who misses another pass. He curses and looks beyond pissed off, but he keeps trying, which I guess is a good thing.

For some reason, the ref blows his whistle, and Coach shouts for a line-up switch.

"The reason I told him I'd think about it is because I actually like him. Which means if we date and for some reason we break up, then I'm guaranteed to be left with a broken heart," Hailey tells us while keeping her eyes on BooBoo.

We should probably be getting the crowd amped up, but I'm pretty sure this conversation is more important right now.

"Giiirrlllll," Rebecca draws out the word. "You can't live your life worrying about a future heartbreak that might not even happen. Live for the now. You like the boy, and he obviously likes you too, so fucking say yes already."

Hailey huffs out a breath but marches her way over to BooBoo and gives his shoulder a shake.

We're too far away to hear what they are saying, but judging by how bright BooBoo is smiling, I'm pretty sure Hailey just made his night. They exchange a few more words, and Hailey kisses his cheek before making her way back to us.

"Hopefully, he can play better now that he's not worried that you were about to turn him down," Rebecca says, but Hailey just rolls her eyes, unable to get rid of the big ass smile on her lips.

"Enough talking; let's get the crowd going," she says and calls for the other cheerleaders to join us.

AS SOON AS Hailey agreed to go out with BooBoo, it was like a fire was lit under his ass, and he played the best I've seen him play all season. Which allowed GSU to walk away with a winning score of five-three.

"You did so good," I tell Rio once we've both changed and had a quick shower.

"Thanks, babe, but I'll admit I was a little nervous we were gonna lose for a bit there."

"So was I. We're pretty sure BooBoo was getting lost in his head because he asked Hailey out, and she told him she needed to think about it."

Rio's brows shoot up and it's like a light bulb goes off in his head. "That makes a lot of sense because after she talked to him was when everything turned around. So, she agreed to go out with him?"

"Yup," I reply with a big grin. "I think they are going to make the cutest couple."

"Not as cute as us, though," he says, squeezing my hand and beaming at me like a lovesick fool. Which I have to admit is my new favorite look on him. He literally looks at me like I hung the stars, and it causes butterflies to erupt in my stomach every time.

As we walk to his car, I force myself not to look around, which is getting easier as each day passes. It's been two weeks since the video went viral, and there have been no signs of Lux, which is what the logical side of my brain has been predicting all along. But that still isn't enough to completely wash my anxiety away.

"Are you ready to have your ass kicked at Mario Kart?" I ask Rio as he drives us to his apartment.

Monster and Bronny are joining us for our video game night tonight, and I even convinced Max to come along. It's going to be great to spend a night with all of our friends.

I've been able to tell a simplified version of my story to all of our friends now, and the way they have rallied around me has left me blown away. I knew I wasn't alone anymore, but they've really shown me just how much I mean to them. They've made sure I'm never left alone if I don't want to be and are always a phone call away if I'm panicking. And they've never once made me feel like I'm stupid for feeling the way I feel. They are really the best people a guy could ask for.

# CHAPTER TWENTY-SIX

## 2 WEEKS LATER

TODAY IS the first day that I've felt brave enough to walk by myself to school, and when I arrived safe and sound, a large portion of my anxiety faded away. If Lux was actually going to hunt me down, he would have done it by now, right?

Since there were two soccer games this week, finding a time to fit Carter into my schedule was a little harder than usual, but we're both free today, and we made a plan to meet up after classes.

"Ready to show me your Fouetté?" I ask Carter when he gets to the room we're using for the next hour.

He groans, and I can't help but smile. "Do I really have to?" he asks, and I nod.

"Absolutely, and we are going to keep practicing it this entire hour until you get it right."

"You're a sadist, aren't you?" he questions with a fake glare.

I shrug. "Maybe."

He sighs, and I laugh before pressing play on my phone, filling the room with music that's set up to play through my Bluetooth speaker.

BY THE TIME we're done with our lesson, we are both sweaty messes because, of course, I allowed him to coax me into dancing a few songs with him like I do every time we get together.

"Now I'm tired and sore," I murmur as we walk down the hall.

"Welcome to my world," Carter retorts.

"Yes, but you pay me to teach you how to dance. Teach being the keyword. I shouldn't have to dance that hard too."

"I didn't tell you to go as hard as you did. That's all on you," he replies with a smirk, and I roll my eyes.

When we get to my exit, I tell him goodnight, and I start my journey home. The air has a chill to it, which is to be expected since it's already November, but it's not unbearable. Although it does make me miss the warmer weather I grew up with, a gust of wind rushes past me, sending a shiver down my spine, making me zip my coat up all the way and pull the collar up to protect my neck. Stupid Michigan weather.

As I walk, I keep my senses on high alert, paying attention to my surroundings. Even though I am feeling braver, that small underlying anxiety is still there and won't let me relax.

The streets are quiet tonight, like they usually are, since we don't live on a main street, and I've barely seen any cars or people walking about. That should put my mind at ease, but it does the exact opposite for some reason.

I'm only about a block away from my house when my phone vibrates in my pocket, pulling my attention away from my anxiety. When I pull it out, a sense of calm and peace rushes over me, and a giant smile spreads across my face as I see Rio's name on the screen.

Rio: Are you home yet? I'm on my way to
your place now.

> Me: Almost! I'm about a block away.

Rio: Taking the same path as always?

> Me: You know it!

Rio: Perfect. We'll probably arrive at the
same time then.

> Me: Sounds good to me. Carter convinced
> me to show him a routine I haven't done in
> YEARS. Think you can give me a massage
> and work out some of these knots.

Rio: An excuse to get my hands all over your
body? Yes, please!

I smile even wider, and a warm sash wraps around my heart squeezing it gently as butterflies dance in my stomach. Rio is the best man I've ever met, and I'm pretty sure I'm in love with him. That has to be what this feeling is.

"Hello, Nathaniel," an all too familiar voice says, causing the smile to slip from my face and my entire body to freeze.

It's like my veins are filled with ice water. My brain is screaming for me to run but I physically can't move.

"You shouldn't be here," I whisper to Lux. He finally comes into my path of vision, holding a gun with a shaky hand, which causes my stomach to drop and my breath to catch. How the hell did he get a gun, and is he unhinged enough to use it?

He looks like shit. Nothing like the man he was when we were together. But it has been seven years, and I know I've changed too.

His clothes are wrinkled like he's been sleeping in the same outfit for a couple of days. His hair is on the longer side and a complete mess. His skin, which used to have a warm sun-kissed glow, is now almost grey. And even though he was always on the slimmer side, he now looks frail, like he could break in half at any moment. The years have not been good to him, and that has me even more terrified.

"You're wrong about that," he says with a venomous tone. "I'm exactly where I should be. I made a promise to you years ago, and I'm here to follow through on it."

I take a shaky breath and a few tears trickle down my face.

"You don't have to do that," I say with a soft soothing voice I used to use when we fought.

Lux cackles at my words and shakes his. "Again, you're wrong." He sneers, taking a step toward me, causing me to shake. "You ruined my fucking life. I have nothing thanks to you. You took away my money, my job, and all the joy I had in life. And here you are, living a happy little life with your soccer boyfriend. You don't deserve to be happy. You don't deserve to live. You knew what would happen if you left me. It might have taken me seven years to find you, but I'm here now, and I'm going to make good on that promise I made when we were together."

He moves his finger to the trigger, and I close my eyes, thinking about Rio and everything that Lux could take away from me right now if he so chose to.

"Looks like somethings never change," Lux says as tears stream down my face. "Here, I thought that you might have actually gained a backbone over the years. I was expecting a fight, but I should have known you'd still be the spineless pussy you always were."

*You can't give up.* A voice in my head tells me. *You aren't alone anymore. You have so much to live for. This isn't how you go. You need to fight. You never fought back before because you believed you deserved what he was doing to you. He was also bigger and stronger than you, but he isn't anymore. And you know your worth. You have people who love you. Fight for them. DON'T GIVE UP!*

I open my eyes and glare at Lux. I took everything he did to me and never once stood up for myself. If I'm going to die today, then I'm not going down without a fight.

"Oh, there is some fire in you," he says with a sinister grin.

"The reason your life is pathetic is because of you," I spit the words out at him. My voice is loud and a lot steadier than I thought it would be. "You got what you deserved, and so did I. The life I have now is one I should have always had. You preyed on a young, troubled boy. You exploited my weaknesses and broke me even more than I already was. You turned me into your little puppet. But I'm not a little boy anymore, and I will not let you win this time."

I bare my teeth at him, and I'm pretty sure I surprise both of us when I charge toward him. Even though I was tired from my dance lesson with Carter, the adrenaline that shoots through my veins gives me a speed I didn't even know I had. With a grunt, I slam into his torso, throwing him to the ground and smiling as he loses his grip on the gun. I've never been a fighter, but it's like natural instincts take over, and I start landing blow after blow to his face.

A car screeches to a stop on the street beside us, but I barely pay it any attention, refusing to stop. Because if I do, that will give Lux the chance to grab his gun again, and then I really might lose this fight.

"Sasha!" Rio shouts, sounding beyond panicked, but I still don't stop.

My fists sting as I drive them into Lux's face over and over again, and I don't even think I realize that he's not moving until Rio is shaking my shoulder.

"Stop," he tells me in a firm but soft voice.

I shake my head with tears streaming down my face. "He has a gun. If I stop, he'll kill me."

"He's out cold, baby. He won't hurt you," he tells me, and I finally stop my punches but don't move off Lux just yet.

Rio moves toward the gun and kicks it out into the street so that even if Lux woke up, he wouldn't be able to reach it. When he returns to my side, he wraps his arms around me and slowly lifts me up. I immediately turn in his hold and bury my face into his chest, sobbing uncontrollably.

A siren blares in the night air, and I jump at the sound.

"You called the cops?" I ask him, but he shakes his head.

"Hands in the air," the cop yells, and Rio lets me go so we can obey the orders.

"That boy there is the victim," an older lady says, running out of her home in a house coat and curlers. "I'm the one who called you. I was about to shut my curtains when I saw that man." She points towards Lux's lifeless body. "Pull a gun on this sweet boy. I witnessed the entire thing."

An ambulance pulls up at that moment and the para-medics rush to Lux's aid.

"Okay, I'm going to need all of your statements," the police officer tells us, and I nod.

"I can go first," the woman offers. "Give that poor boy a moment to collect his thoughts."

I mouth thank you at her, and when Rio once again wraps his arms around me, I melt into his embrace.

"Let's sit," he suggests, guiding me to the curb.

"I thought I was going to die," I tell him, watching the paramedics load Lux into the ambulance and drive off. My body is shaking violently as the adrenaline starts to wear off, and my stomach rolls, threatening to empty its contents.

"But you didn't," Rio reminds me. "You fought, and you won. I'm so fucking proud of you, baby."

"I never fought back before," I tell him. "He used to be so much stronger than me, but he wasn't this time. I was ready to give up, but there was this voice in my head that begged me not to. It reminded me that I'm no longer the weak boy I once was." I pause and stare at the night sky for a moment. "I think it was my mom."

"I've heard stories of people swearing their loved ones talked to them from beyond the grave in times of need, so I believe you."

There he goes being the perfect man again.

"I love you," I tell him, knowing that now is the perfect time to get those words off my chest.

He beams at me, then presses his lips to mine. "I love you too, baby… so fucking much."

I wrap my arms around his neck and kiss him like my life depends on it. I could have died tonight, but I didn't, and now I get to live out the happily ever after I wasn't sure I deserved.

The clearing of a throat causes us to pull away and look up at the police officer. "I'm sorry to interrupt, but I'd like to take your statements now."

I nod and grab Rio's hand. "Is it okay if we stay together while giving our statements?" I request.

"I don't see why not," the officer says as we stand up.

I thank him and take a deep breath before telling the entire story. By the time I'm done, the adrenaline has almost completely left my body, and I'm exhausted.

"I didn't see much," Rio admits when it's his turn to give his statement. "When I arrived, Sasha was on top of Lux, punching him. I got him to stop, then kicked the gun away just in case Lux woke up."

The cop nods while making notes.

"I'm going to head to the hospital now and see how Mr. Vanderbilt is doing and get his statement if possible. I'll be in touch with you tomorrow to see how we are going to progress," he tells us once he's done writing everything down.

"Am I going to be in trouble?" I ask a new fear causing me to shake.

The officer shakes his head. "I highly doubt that, son. With the statements I received today, it's evident you were acting in self-defense. The man had a gun, and had you not acted, you very well could have ended up dead tonight. But I'll have more information for you in the morning."

"Thank you," I reply, then turn toward the old lady's house and walk up the path to her door. She answers quickly after I knock and smiles at me in that sweet grandma way. "Thank you for calling the police and for being a witness for me," I tell her.

She waves her hand at me. "I'm just glad I was at the right place at the right time. I was in an abusive relationship once, so I know how hard it is to get out. When I saw the gun, I opened my window, so I heard everything both of you said. That man is foul, and I hope he dies," she says firmly, catching me off guard. You don't expect old ladies to say things like that. "But you're not like him. I've lived in this house for fifty years, and I've seen you walk by countless times. I've seen you help children who have fallen off their bikes or kicked a ball into the street and you retrieve it for them without them asking. I saw you help my neighbor with her garden last year, and you mowed Mr. Hunter's lawn every week this summer while he was recovering from hip surgery. You are a good man, and I'm so glad you stood your ground."

Her words have me tearing up again, and I rush forward to wrap my arms around her. "Thank you," I whisper into her ear.

She rubs my back and shushes me. "No thanks is needed. It's what neighbors do for each other."

"Well, I appreciate it more than you'll ever know," I tell her.

"Have a good night, boys. If you need anything, please don't hesitate to ask."

We agree and wave at her as we leave.

"Come on, let's get you to bed," Rio says, helping me into his car.

I smile at him and nod. I'm pretty sure I'm going to pass out the second my head hits the pillow. Which is fine by me, I'm ready to put this day behind me.

When we get to my house, we strip out of our clothing and climb into my bed. As predicted, I'm asleep almost instantly, in the arms of the man who loves me.

# CHAPTER TWENTY-SEVEN

## Sasha

MY HEART IS RACING as I wait for Officer Lettermen to bring me into his office. He called me early this morning and told me it would be best if I came down to the precinct. Even though I know I'm innocent and he told me I didn't have anything to worry about last night, I still decided to call up one of my professors and ask him if he knew someone who could represent me.

Being a law student teaches you that you should really never speak to a police officer without a lawyer present. Of course, I didn't think about that last night when I gave my initial report because I wasn't in the best state of mind. But today, my thoughts are much clearer, and I knew I needed to make a call. Thankfully, my professor has a friend who was able to take me on at the last minute. I gave Mr. Cox the brief rundown of everything, and he was certain that no matter what happened today I wouldn't be in any trouble, but of course, it was best that he came along just in case.

"It's going to be fine," he assures me when my knee won't stop shaking.

I nod, but his words don't do much to settle my nerves. If everything was okay, why did I have to come to the precinct? If nothing was going to happen, wouldn't they have just told me that over the phone?

I'm not sure how long we wait before Officer Lettermen

comes out and greets me. "Thank you for coming in, Mr. Lawrence," he says, and I shake his hand.

"It's not a problem at all. This is my lawyer Mr. Cox, he'll be joining us for our conversation today."

Officer Lettermen tilts his head to the side. "Why did you bring a lawyer?" he questions with a lifted brow.

"Because it's my right," I reply.

The officer presses his lips together but nods and leads us to a small room.

"Care to tell us what this meeting is about?" Mr. Cox asks Officer Lettermen. "If you are just going to ask if my client wants to press charges, the answer is yes."

"I'm afraid that won't be possible," Officer Lettermen replies. "Mr. Vanderbilt was pronounced dead when he arrived at the hospital last night."

I gasp, but Mr. Cox puts his hand out, reminding me not to say anything. "I'm sorry to hear that," he tells the officer. "But as I'm sure you're aware, Michigan has a stand-your-ground law. Mr. Vanderbilt had a gun and was holding it in my client's face. My client had every right to take Mr. Vander-bilt down, and if he passed away due to those injuries, that is unfortunate, but there are no charges you can hold my client on."

Officer Lettermen pushes his tongue into his upper lip, looking slightly annoyed, but nods. "Yes, I am aware of that I just wanted to go over Mr. Lawrence's statement one more time since Mr. Vanderbilt wasn't able to give his."

It's sketchy that he said there was nothing to worry about and now is wanting more. I'm really fucking glad now that I brought a lawyer.

"You can read it out loud to us if you'd like, but my client won't be saying anything more," Mr. Cox answers for me.

Officer Lettermen huffs out a breath through his nose and then dips his chin. "Okay, well, that's all I need then."

"Excellent, you have a good afternoon," Mr. Cox says

before nodding at me to stand. I do exactly that and follow him out. "What a slimy fucking guy," he grumbles once we're outside. "I can guarantee he was going to try and get you to confess to murder."

I nod. "I clued in on that too. I'm glad I made the right decision to call Professor Lymus this morning."

"I'm glad I was available to take you on," he responds. "It makes me sick when officers want to take advantage of people. You went through hell because of Lux Vanderbilt, yet that stupid cop still wanted to see you behind bars."

"Can we work out a payment plan?" I ask him, but he shakes his head.

"No need, kid, it's pro bono."

"Are you sure?" I check, and he nods.

"Absolutely," he assures me. "Your professor is a good man and has helped me out too many times to count. The least I could do is keep one of his students out of jail. What you can do as payment is continue working your ass off and pass the bar when it's your time."

I smile widely at him. "That I can do. I want to help people who have been where I am. The system far too often fails those in domestic abuse situations."

"When you graduate, give me a call," he tells me. "I think my office could use a guy like you. Obviously we can't hire you on as a lawyer until you pass your bar exam and get admitted to that bar, but you could work as a law clerk until all of that happens. It would be a great way for you to get your foot in the door and help you network with established professionals in the legal field. I'd also be on board to mentor you during that time."

My brows shoot up, and I quickly bobbly my head in acceptance. There's no way I'm turning down that offer. "Thank you so much," I gush, and he smiles at me before handing me his card even though I already have his number.

"I look forward to working with you," he tells me. Then

we say our goodbyes, and I head off to where Rio is waiting for me.

"How did it go?" he checks when I get in the car.

"Lux is dead," I tell him, and his eyes go wide.

"Holy shit," he whispers.

"That's exactly how I felt when I heard the news. I'm really glad I brought Mr. Cox with me because we're pretty sure Officer Lettermen was going to try and arrest me for murder."

"But it was self-defense!" Rio shouts.

I smile at him and place my hand on his knee. "Exactly, and thanks to Michigan having a stand-your-ground law there were no charges he could press against me. But if I didn't have a lawyer, he definitely would have tried to get me to talk and confess to something that wasn't true."

Rio shakes his head. "That's fucking crazy."

"That's the world we live in. I really hope one day I get to help someone the way Mr. Cox just helped me. He actually kind of offered me a job once I graduate."

"Holy shit," Rio replies with a toothy grin. "That's amazing, baby. You deserve it. You are an amazing man, and you're going to be an even better lawyer."

"I love you," I reply, leaning over the console for a quick kiss.

"I love you too. Now let me get you home so you can rest," he says, but I shoot him my best *'are you serious?'* look.

"I don't have time to rest. I have to get my shit packed so we don't miss the bus that leaves in less than thirty minutes," I tell him.

"You're still coming to the game?" he asks, and I roll my eyes as I nod.

"Did you lose some brain cells last night? Of course I'm coming to the game. I'm the team's good luck charm. I can't let them down."

"I think they would understand due to the circumstances

of what just happened to you," he replies, but I give my head a firm shake.

"I don't care. I'm going. Yes, I could have died last night, but I didn't. Lux is gone, and I can finally move on with my life. He no longer has a hold on me, and I couldn't be more grateful. Staying at home makes no sense to me. It's time to live and appreciate everything the universe has given to me."

Rio gives me a passionate kiss before whispering against my lips, "You are so fucking amazing."

The past twenty-four hours have been horrible and amazing at the same time. I'm finally free of the dark shadow that has been haunting me for the last seven years. Never again can Lux Vanderbilt hurt me.

# CHAPTER TWENTY-EIGHT

COACH RUDDER IS GLARING at Sasha and me when we arrive at the bus five minutes late.

"Sorry, Coach, it's my fault we were late," Sasha tells him. "My crazy ex showed up last night and held me at gunpoint. I was able to catch him off guard and knock him to the ground, but I guess when I was punching him, I went too hard, and he ended up dying. The officer who was on the scene last night pulled me in for more questioning this morning, and I think he was trying to arrest me for murder. Thankfully, I'm a smart law student and brought a lawyer along, and no charges were laid, but it caused me to get behind on my packing, so that's why we're late." The words tumble out of Sasha's lips so quickly I'm positive Coach doesn't have time to process them as he looks like a deer caught in the headlights. "I promise it won't happen again," Sasha assures him.

Coach blinks a few times, clearly trying to process everything Sasha just said, but eventually shrugs. "You're probably going to have to tell the whole story to Evangeline and a couple of other people, but we don't have time for that right now, so get on the bus," he instructs, and he quickly does as we're told.

"Look who finally decided to grace us with their presence," BooBoo says as we grab our seats in the row across from him and Hailey.

"I almost got arrested I think that grants me a five-minute pardon," Sasha sasses him, causing his brows to shoot up.

"Spill the tea," Hailey says, leaning over with a glint in her eye.

"Later," Sasha replies. "I'm tired and need a nap."

"You're no fun," the cheerleader says, then sticks her tongue out at Sasha.

"Love you too," he tells her with a wink.

"You know you don't owe anyone the story if you don't want to tell it," I whisper to Sasha as he leans his head on my shoulder.

He offers me the sweetest smile in return. "I know, but now that Lux is gone, it's like this weight I didn't even know I was carrying is lifted off my shoulders. I'm free. Telling people about how I stuck up for myself isn't going to be hard at all."

I kiss his forehead, loving just how resilient he is.

WHEN WE ARRIVE at the hotel, it's shortly after eight, and everyone heads directly to their rooms. There's an earlier curfew tonight since we need our rest for the game tomorrow, but we still have about an hour before we're stuck in our rooms for the night, so once BooBoo and I have dropped our bags off, we make our way to Hailey and Sasha's room.

We considered BooBoo and Sasha switching rooms for the night, but Coach made it mighty clear that he will be doing room checks tonight, and we all better be in the right places. I guess that's what happens when there are two couples on the team.

"Okay, are you finally going to tell us what the hell happened last night," Hailey says once we're all sitting on the beds.

"Lux showed up," Sasha starts, and Hailey gasps.

He nods and then tells our friends the entire story. When he finally finishes, Hailey has tears in her eyes and jumps forward to give Sasha a big hug.

"I'm sorry that happened, but I'm glad you're finally free," she tells him.

"Me too," he replies. "I guess my tarot reading was really accurate, though. It predicted the chaos, but it also told me good luck would be coming my way, which I think is already happening. My lawyer pretty much offered me a job once I pass the bar."

Hailey shrieks and squeezes Sasha one more time. "You deserve it, sweetie."

A knock comes on the door, and we all sigh. "Guess it's time to head back to our room," BooBoo grumbles, and I nod.

We both give our partners a quick kiss before opening the door. Coach is standing there with a knowing smile on his lips. "Time for bed, guys," he tells us, and we slowly trudge to our room.

I know it's only one night apart, but I miss Sasha already.

As I'm about to climb into bed, a gentle knock comes from the door. When I open it, Sasha is standing there with a shy smile, and I quickly let him in so he doesn't get spotted.

"Hailey and I came up with an agreement that we're going to take turns sleeping in here. That way if middle of the night room checks are done, it's easier to cover instead of two people being in the wrong rooms."

I smile and pull him in for a gentle kiss. "Well, I'm glad you got the first night I was really not looking forward to sleeping without you tonight."

"Remember the rule, guys. I'm not above dousing you in ice water," BooBoo reminds us, and we laugh before pulling apart and climbing into bed.

"Night, BooBoo," Sasha says once we shut the lights off.

"Goodnight," he replies, and I swear I can hear the smile in his voice.

I'm so thankful I have surrounded myself with amazing people.

# CHAPTER TWENTY-NINE

EVANGELINE LOOKS COMPLETELY SHOCKED as I tell her my story of an abusive ex, almost dying, and then almost getting arrested.

"Jesus, that's a lot," she murmurs once I'm finished.

"Tell me about it."

"But you're no longer in any legal trouble?" she checks, and I nod.

"My lawyer did a fantastic job at letting the police know that I'm well represented and know my rights, so I doubt they'll try anything more. And as far as I know, Lux doesn't have any family that is going to come for me. He told me he was an orphan when we were together, and he didn't have any siblings."

"Okay, well if anything does come up, just let me know. I'll have your back no matter what, and I'll try to keep the school on your side if possible," she assures me.

"I appreciate it," I tell her, not feeling worried about anything more coming up.

Lux was a fantastic liar, but I'm pretty sure if he actually had a support system, I would have known about it or at least suspected it. But my gut is telling me that I'm finally in the clear.

"Would you like some time off to deal with everything that happened?" she inquires, but I shake my head.

"I'm good," I assure her. "Besides, I don't think the team and their superstitions would appreciate that."

She shrugs. "I could probably get one of the other team members to take your place."

"Don't worry about it. I really am good. Better than I have been in a long time," I tell her honestly.

She smiles, accepting my answer. "I'm glad to hear that. I can't imagine what it must have been like to go through what you did, but I'm glad you came out stronger on the other side. You are an amazing person, and I'm so glad we were able to meet."

"Being a mascot wasn't something I ever thought I would do, but I'm so glad I stumbled upon it because it changed my life for the better. I've made amazing friendships, and getting to travel with my boyfriend is a plus."

"Speaking of that," she says with a lifted brow. "Coach Rudder has filled me in about you sneaking into rooms after curfew."

I sigh but decide not to deny it. "I don't understand why it's a big deal. Honestly, I think he should just let me and BooBoo trade room assignments. We're all adults, so why can't we be in a room with our partners? I could see it being a big deal if BooBoo or Rio stopped performing as well as they are, but get us to sign an agreement or something saying that we'll accept the original room assignments if performance tanks."

Evangeline eyes me for a moment but eventually shrugs. "I'll talk with the coach and the management teams, but I can't see where you're wrong. In the meantime, try to be sneakier," she tells me, and I laugh.

"You've got it," I reply with a salute. We say our good-byes, and I leave her office with the promise that we'll hopefully have new room assignments for our next away game on Sunday.

"HOW DID your chat with Evangeline go?" Rio asks when I arrive at his apartment.

The day flew by crazy fast, and I can't believe it's already time for our date. We've been dating for a little over five weeks now and have only gone out together without friends once. I decided that wasn't good enough, so last night, I started coming up with a plan for us to do something fun.

"Really good. She told me she has my back, and she's even going to try to get our room assignments changed. But we are all going to have to sign agreements that say we won't allow this to affect anyone's performance on the pitch," I inform him with a bright smile.

He pulls me into his arms and plants a perfect kiss on my lips. "Have I told you how amazing you are recently?"

"Yes, but I won't turn down hearing it more often," I reply with a smirk.

He chuckles and then kisses me again.

"Aww, you two are too cute," Monster says, coming out of his room.

"We are, aren't we," I reply with a wink.

"Are you guys sticking around, or are you heading out on another date?" he checks.

"Another date. It was my turn to plan something awesome."

"Does that mean you have no idea what you're going to do?" Monster asks Rio, who nods.

"Yup, but I don't mind. I'm just happy to be spending time with the man I love."

Is he trying to turn me into a puddle of goo? Because if he is, it's mission accomplished.

"Well, you two have fun, and don't be too loud when you get back," Monster says, making Rio blush.

"We could always go back to my place," I whisper to Rio, who shrugs.

"You have roommates too," he reminds me.

"Yeah, but you don't have to see them every day, and I could give two shits if they hear us enjoying ourselves."

He shakes his head at my antics, then gives me another quick kiss.

"How did I fall in love with someone like you?"

I shove his shoulder gently. "I'm amazing, and you know it. Now come on, we don't want to be late," I say, grabbing his hand and dragging him out the door.

He snatches his jacket quickly and puts it on as we make our way to the elevator.

When we get to Rio's car, I pull up the address to our destination on my phone and begin to give him directions.

"You're really holding on to the whole surprise thing," Rio notes as he drives.

"It's more fun this way," I reply before telling him to make a left.

It doesn't take us long to arrive at our destination but the smile that's on my man's lips lets me know I made the right call.

"A comedy club?" he questions.

"Laughter is the best medicine, and I think after what we've been through this weekend, we deserve all the laughter in the world."

"Can't argue with that kind of logic," he says as we get out of the car.

A warm and inviting energy wraps around my body as we walk toward the front doors, hand in hand. I know it's the love that we feel for each other, and I'm never going to let it go.

# CHAPTER THIRTY

THE COMEDY CLUB was an amazing experience, but I'm excited to get Sasha back to my room and be alone with him.

We've been messing around a lot and have found so many different ways to get off, but we haven't had sex yet, and I'm hoping tonight we can make that change. Sasha keeps making comments about taking my giant cock, so I know he's on board. I've been the apprehensive one.

Thankfully, Monster and Bronny are both in their rooms when we get back to my apartment, so I don't have to face my friends' ribbing.

Once my bedroom door is shut, I grab Sasha and smash our lips together, pressing him against the door.

"I need you," I whisper against his lips before diving in for more. "Want to be inside you," I tell him as I trail kisses along his jaw and down his neck.

"Really?" Sasha squeaks the word out, and I grind my hard cock into his hip in response.

"I know we've been taking our time, but I'm ready," I assure him, stepping back to take my jacket off and pull my shirt over my head.

"Fuck, I've been waiting for you to say those words," he replies, quickly stripping out of his own clothes.

"Get on the bed on all fours," I instruct, not missing the way Sasha's eyes light up at my bossy side.

"Yes, Sir," he practically purrs the words before strutting toward the bed and assuming the position.

I take a deep breath as I stare at Sasha's perfect body. His strong legs and arms hold him in place, and his back gently rises and falls with each breath. His delicious cock hangs heavy between his legs, already hard as a rock.

Licking my lips, I step toward him, then kneel between his legs and use my hands to spread his cheeks apart.

"So fucking perfect," I whisper before leaning forward and trailing my tongue across his pucker.

"God," he cries out in a breathy tone, his head lifting back as he does, which results in his spine curving down.

"You like that baby?" I inquire before swirling my tongue around his star again.

"Ungh," he responds, and I can't help but chuckle at his nonsense.

"You taste so fucking good," I tell him before stiffening my tongue, shoving it through the tight muscles of his entrance. "I don't think I'm ever going to get enough of you."

I suck on my fingers before returning to enjoy the delicious taste of my man. As I eat his ass, I gently slide in one finger alongside my tongue and smile as his needy moans and whimpers get louder. He eventually drops his head to the bed to bite my comforter and muffle his noises. We really need a night alone where we don't have to worry about being too loud.

I take my time stretching Sasha with my tongue and fingers, knowing that I'm not small and I really don't want to hurt him.

"I need you," Sasha begs, but I shake my head.

"Not yet. I want to make sure you're good and stretched," I tell him, then slide my fingers out, not missing the way he whimpers at the loss. "It's okay, baby. I'm going to take good care of you, but I want you to flip over."

While he gets into position, I open my nightstand drawer and grab the bottle of lube and a condom. I don't need the condom just yet, but the second he's ready, I'm going to want to be balls deep inside him, and I won't want to stop to grab the proper supplies.

"Grab the backs of your thighs and show me that gorgeous pucker," I tell him as I pour a generous amount of lube onto my fingers.

My man obeys instantly, and I bite my lower lip at how perfectly he's presenting himself to me.

Slowly I slide three fingers inside him while trailing kisses down his leg toward his leaking cock.

"Shit, that feels so good," Sasha moans out as I continue to stretch him. "But I need your cock."

"Soon, baby," I assure him. "I don't want to hurt you."

He shakes his head, his beautiful hair rubbing against the bed and sprawling out around him like a halo. "You won't hurt me. I promise. I like the burn. Please just fuck me already."

"One more finger," I tell him, pressing my pinky in along with the other fingers.

"F-f-fuuuckkkk," he cries out, his eyes rolling into the back of his head.

"God, you look so good with my fingers inside you," I tell him as I pump them in and out of his tight channel.

"N-n-need… yoooou," he pants the words out, and I decide that I also can't wait any longer.

Carefully I pull my fingers out, then sheath myself in the condom and pour more lube onto my cock before positioning myself at his entrance.

"Ready, baby?" I check while holding myself tightly at the base.

As soon as he nods, I begin to inch myself inside of him, taking my time and allowing his body to get used to my size.

"Holy fucking shit," he moans out as I slowly enter him.

His hole is so fucking tight that it's literally choking my cock, almost making it hard to breathe.

"More," he pleads when I pause, and I can't keep back the groan that slips past my lips as I push in farther and farther until I'm all the way in.

My heart races, and I lean forward to kiss my man.

"How are you doing?" I check once I've caught my breath.

"Soooo good, but I'm ready for you to fuck me," he informs me like the needy little slut he is.

"I don't think I'm going to last long," I tell him.

"That's okay, neither will I," he replies.

I nod, then kiss him again before pulling my hips back and then slamming into him.

Both of us moan as I find a rhythm, his channel milking me each time I thrust in and out of him. My spine begins to tingle, so I grab hold of his cock and start to jack him off, trying to keep it in rhythm with my thrusts, but as my orgasm draws nearer, it becomes difficult.

"Fuck. Shit. Fuck," Sasha curses as his cock pulses in my fist and thick ropes of cum shoot out, covering his abs and chest.

As his climax takes over his body, he clamps down around me, and it's almost painful how tight his hold becomes on me.

"Jeeeesuusss," I breathe out the word, and my movements become jagged as my own release takes over me.

The orgasm is so intense it literally takes my breath away. Once I'm able to breathe again, I suck in a giant breath of air, gasping a little as I try to fill my lungs again.

My heart is pounding so hard in my chest that I almost wonder if Sasha can hear it.

Both Sasha and I are silent for a few moments; the only sound in the room is our pants.

"I knew that was going to be amazing, but I didn't realize

it was damn near going to kill me," Sasha says once he can talk again.

I chuckle, and Sasha makes a face. I'm not sure what to call it. It's somewhere between a grimace and a confused expression. "Your cock jiggles inside me when you laugh. It's weird and I'm not sure if I like it or not," he tells me, and I can't help but laugh again. He shakes his head, scrunching his nose. "Yeah, I don't think I like it."

Not wanting to cause him any discomfort, I slowly slide out of him, then tie off the condom and throw it in my trash can. Once that's taken care of, I get up and grab the clean towel I placed on my dresser earlier today when I decided this was what I wanted to do. I make my way back to my man who looks blissed out and sleepy and gently clean him up.

"What a gentleman," Sasha murmurs.

I toss the soiled towel in the general direction of my hamper, not caring if it actually makes its way in, and turn off the lights before climbing back into bed with Sasha.

"I love you," I whisper, pulling him into my arms.

"I love you so much it almost scares me," Sasha tells me, and I tilt my head to the side.

"Why would it scare you?" I question, trailing my hand up and down his back as I wait for his response.

"Because I've never experienced a love like this before. I'm afraid I'm going to mess it up."

"That's impossible," I tell him, pressing a kiss to the top of his head. "We're going to have ups and downs, and we'll both make mistakes along the way, but you can't mess up love. You just keep trying every day. As long as you are doing your best and you never stop loving me, then there's nothing to worry about."

Soft lips press against my chest, and the touch shoots directly to my heart, warming it with love.

"Thank you for loving me," he tells me in a soft voice.

"No thanks is needed. I'm going to love you until the day that I die," I vow to him.

"Same," he replies.

I give him a gentle squeeze, letting him know just how much that one word means to me. Forever is a long time, but I think as long as we keep trying, we can make it.

# CHAPTER THIRTY-ONE

## ROUGHLY 1 MONTH LATER

THE COOL AIR fills my lungs as I take a deep inhale and wait for the ball to get back in motion. Today is the championship game, and I refuse to let our team lose. We worked so fucking hard to get here, and I know we have it in us to bring home this last win of the season.

Once the ball is in motion, I run into place and wait for my teammate to make his next move. He makes eye contact with me and then sends the ball flying in my direction. I catch the ball with precision and dribble it farther down the pitch before passing it to BooBoo since I don't have a clear line to the net.

BooBoo dribbles the ball a little further before kicking it with all his might toward the net. I hold my breath as I watch the ball, and when it flies into the net, I shout at the top of my lungs and rush over to my friend, pounding him on the back in celebration.

"That's how it's done," Whiley yells, giving BooBoo a bro hug.

The score is now three-one, and there isn't much time left on the clock. I can practically taste the victory already, but I won't get cocky, that's how games are lost.

I cast a quick glance at Kerrington, who is cheering on the

sidelines, smiling softly for my man before getting into position and staring down my opponents like I do every game. Even though they also look determined, there's a hint of defeat there already. They know how unlikely it is for them to win, but they aren't giving up, which I respect.

Our team gets possession of the ball once it's in play, and I run ahead to secure an open spot. Within seconds, the ball is sent toward me, but I'm almost immediately blocked, so I send it to BooBoo and run farther ahead. He sends the ball back to me, but once again, an opponent is on my ass, so I kick it toward Whiley, who is able to break away, and I internally cheer.

The crowd starts to countdown, and when Whiley sends the ball soaring into the net just as the crowd gets to two, securing our Championship win.

"Yes!" I shout as loud as I possibly can before rushing over to my teammates, who are piling on top of Whiley. "We fucking did! We won. We fucking won!"

Sasha rushes to the field in his Kerrington costume and gives me an awkward hug before grabbing Whiley's hand and holding it up in victory.

"I'm so fucking proud of you," Sasha tells me, but I don't have time to respond before the cheerleaders are joining us, and he has to perform once more.

It doesn't matter to me that we can't celebrate on the pitch together because I know we'll be celebrating later tonight once we're both able to leave.

IT FEELS like forever before I finally have Sasha in my arms and he's giving me the best celebratory kiss ever.

"You guys killed it," he tells me as we break for air.

"I can't believe we actually won," I reply. "This is literally all I ever dreamt about. And now that it's happened, it doesn't even feel real."

"Well, it is real, whether it feels that way to you or not, and I couldn't be more proud of you. You made your own dreams come true, baby; not many people get to say that."

"You're my dream," I tell him, then press my lips to his again.

"Do you know that I practically turn into a puddle of goo every time you talk to me like that?" he asks with a cheesy grin.

"Then my words are doing exactly what I wanted them to do," I reply, giving his lips a quick peck.

"Stop making out it's time to paaaarrtttaaayy," BooBoo tells us, walking in our direction with his arm slung around Hailey's shoulder.

"There are worse ways I could spend my evening," Sasha replies, making Hailey giggle.

"Stop acting put off. You know tonight is going to be a great time," Hailey tells my man, who just shrugs.

"I mean, probably, but when I'm at the party, I'm not getting railed, and that's a lot more fun in my mind," he says, and it's my turn to laugh.

"We could lock ourselves in a bathroom and have a quickie if you want," I whisper into his ears, and when he looks at me, his eyes are filled with lust and a mischievous glint.

"My slutty ways are rubbing off on you. I love it," he says with a waggle of his brows.

"Okay, horn-dogs it's time to go," Hailey states, before skipping off with BooBoo to his car that is parked beside mine.

"If you don't show up, I'll drive to your place and slash your tires," BooBoo warns me as he gets into his car, making Sasha cackle.

"He's really good at threats," my man points out, and I nod.

"And they aren't empty either. When he says something, he follows through."

"Hailey's the same way. Maybe that's why they are so good together," Sasha muses out loud.

The house where the party is being held is about twenty minutes out of town, so it gives Sasha and me plenty of alone time before we have to be social again.

"Have you ever gotten roadhead before?" Sasha asks with a sultry tone.

My brows shoot up, and I slowly shake my head, casting a quick glance at my man, who is licking his lips.

"Then this is going to be so much fun," he says, unbuckling his seat belt and leaning over the console.

"I-I-I don't think this is safe," I stammer as he unbuttons my jeans and shoves my underwear down just enough to free my cock.

"Just keep your eyes on the road, baby, and I'll do all the work," he assures me before taking me into his warm, wet mouth.

I suck in a quick breath, tightening my grip on the steering wheel, trying to stop my eyes from rolling into the back of my head.

"Mmmm you taste so good," Sasha tells me while lapping at my throbbing cock like it's a lollipop.

I wasn't hard when we started this drive, but I went from soft to rock hard in a matter of seconds. The instant his mouth was on my dick, it fully came to life, craving more of his touch and talented tongue.

Sasha has been working on his deep throating abilities since I'm apparently a lot larger than anyone he's been with before, and he's told me that he's determined to get all of me in his mouth one day. He hasn't managed to do that just yet, but I'm more than happy to let him practice.

"Your mouth is dangerous," I tell him, gasping when he starts to bob up and down.

His hums of pleasure send jolts directly through my cock and up my spine, making it harder to keep my eyes open and focused on the road.

Sasha's hands join the mix, and I have no idea how long I'm going to last. I think the reason I'm so close to coming already is a mixture of the toe-curling pleasure my man is giving me right now and the adrenaline of how it's being done. I've never done anything like this in my life, and I probably never would have if I'd never started dating Sasha. He's always pushing me out of my comfort zone and getting me to try new things. He also revealed a side of myself I didn't even know existed.

I knew that I had to connect with someone to feel sexual desire, but I didn't know that with the right person, that feeling could be intensified to the level that I feel with Sasha. Even with past partners, I didn't want to have sex as much as I do with my sexy minx. He's lit a fire inside of me and I pray it never gets extinguished.

"I think I'm ready to take you all the way down my throat," Sasha tells me, pausing for a moment to catch his breath.

Before I even have a chance to respond, my man is lowering himself onto my cock again, relaxing his jaw and fully taking me in.

"F-f-fuck," I stammer out when his nose nestles against my pubes, and he swallows around me, his throat constricting and damn near causing me to get lightheaded.

It only takes one more swallow and another tight pulse around my cock for me to shout and come like a fucking guizer.

Sasha comes up a little so he can breathe, but he doesn't let a single drop of cum escape his thick lips. He keeps sucking me until I'm dry and an over-sensitive mess before popping off and kissing the tip of my cock. He helps shove me back into my underwear before sitting back in his seat and buckling up once again.

"That was so much fun," Sasha notes with a mischievous smile.

"As soon as we get to that party, I'm blowing you in a bathroom," is my response, which has my gorgeous man cackling.

"I like the way you think."

It isn't long after my amazing blow job that we arrive at the party, where BooBoo and Hailey are waiting outside for us.

"Did you become a grandma overnight or something? How come you were driving so slow?" BooBoo asks after we get out of my car.

"Rio just got a little bit distracted," Sasha tells him but the sexy smirk on his lips damn near gives him away. "But if you'll excuse us, I really need to use the bathroom." Sasha grabs my hand, dragging me into the house and I laugh the entire way.

This man is everything I could have wanted in a partner and more. I know that one day I'm going to ask him to spend the rest of his life with me.

# EPILOGUE

## ROUGHLY 15 MONTHS LATER

TODAY HAS BEEN one of the best days of my life and I can't wait until I get home to the man of my dreams so I can tell him all about it. It was my first day at Dover, Cox, and Associates law firm as a lawyer and not just a law clerk, and it went better than I could have imagined.

I'm exactly where I wanted to be in life but some days it still feels like a dream. I've got an amazing man who loves me, a cozy little house, and a job that is not only going to pay well but challenge me in the best ways possible. It's more than I ever could have hoped for. And no, I haven't left dance behind, I'm back to being a part-time instructor at Green Spring Dance Academy teaching one class a week.

When I pull into the driveway of the home Rio and I have been renting, there is a giant smile on my face. How is this really my life? As I walk through the door, I'm greeted with a heavenly aroma that has my mouth watering. I wasn't expecting Rio to cook tonight since we both worked, but there's no way I'm turning down food.

"Whatcha making?" I ask, leaning against the doorframe to the kitchen and taking in just how amazing my man looks in his grey slacks and tan sweater. He's the teacher we all dream about having, that has all the girls and boys drooling over him.

"Lasagna and Caesar salad," he tells me with a toothy grin.

"When did you have time to make all of that?" I question, walking over to him for my welcome home kiss.

"Would you hold it against me if I told you it's all store-bought, and I just had to warm it in the oven?" he asks, then pulls me into his arms and kisses me like he hasn't seen me in days, not hours.

I melt into him, opening my lips eagerly when his tongue licks at the seam requesting entrance. My cock slowly comes to life as we make out in the middle of our kitchen.

"The only thing I'm ever going to hold against you is my body," I tease when we break for air. "How long is the lasagna going to take? Do we have time for a quicky?" I waggle my brows at him, and he chuckles while shaking his head.

"As much as I'd *love* that there won't be time. My alarm should honestly be going off any second," he tells me, and his phone beeps at that very second.

I huff out a breath and pout. "We could always reheat it later," I suggest but of course, Rio doesn't give in.

"Go sit, I'll bring your plate in a minute."

I sigh but do as I'm told. When I turn around the corner to the nook that houses our kitchen table my mouth drops at the beautiful setting, flowers, and candles.

"Baby, you didn't have to do this," I tell him in awe of just how amazing he is.

"I wanted us to celebrate your first day as a lawyer," he says, placing the plates of food on the table. "I also was hoping we could celebrate one more thing."

"What?" I question. When I turn to face him, I gasp and cover my mouth, tears immediately springing to my eyes as I take him in on one knee.

"I'd like to celebrate us taking the next step in our journey together," he starts. "I knew early on in our dating that I wanted to spend the rest of my life with you and I'm hoping you feel the same way too. I don't ever want to live a life that you aren't a part of. You're my everything and I would be honored if you would be my husband."

I'm at a loss for words so I just nod and allow Rio to slide the ring on my finger.

"I love you so much," I whisper once I can somewhat speak again. "I can't wait to marry you."

Rio stands and pulls me in for a passionate, love-filled kiss.

I'm the luckiest man alive right now. I get to spend the rest of my life with a man who loves me more than words can say and who will never treat me the way I was treated in the past. He's my everything and he makes me a better man. I know my mom would be proud and honored to call Rio her son-in-law. And I also know that she would love the man I turned into with the help of the love of my life.

Forever is a long time, but I know it will be amazing with Rio by my side.

**The End**

*Thank you so much for reading Teasing the Winger! If you loved this story please leave an honest review!*

***Up next we have Carter and Brendon in - Winning the Point Guard:*** *an m/m, best friends to lovers, bi-awakening, college basketball romance.*

*Coming to Amazon and Kindle Unlimited Sept 26th. Pre-Order Today.*

LAURA JOHN

# ALSO BY LAURA JOHN

## GSU - M/M COLLEGE SPORTS SERIES

1. Schooling the Quarterback: (An M/M Tutor/Athlete Football Romance) ***

2. Testing the Goalie: (An M/M Professor/Student Hockey Romance) ***

3. Teasing the Winger: (An M/M Annoyances to Lovers Soccer Romance) ***

4. Winning the Point Guard: (An M/M, friends to lovers, bi-awakening, basketball romance) ***

## HUNTER SECURITY SERIES

1. **Nixon: (An m/m bodyguard romance)** ***

2. **Denver: (An m/m best friends to lovers, single dad romance)** ***

3. **Knox: (A Suspenseful M/M Brother's Best Friend Romance)** ***

4. **Bennett: (An m/m bodyguard romance)** ***

## SULTRY SUMMER SERIES

1. Summer Heat (A FREE small town romance short story)

2. Long Summer Nights (A Small town low angst romance)

3. Summer Daze (A Small Town Interracial romance)

4. **Summer Memories (A M/M second chance romance)*****

5. **Summer Dreams (A M/M Age Gap romance)*****

## LOVE IN SIENNA SERIES

1. Secret Smiles (A friends to lovers rock star romance) *ALSO AVAILABLE IN AUDIO!*

2. Hidden Kisses (An enemies to lovers baseball romance)

3. Guarded Hearts (A best friends to lovers, single mother romance)

4. Whispered Desires (A single mother, enemies to lovers, age gap, rock star romance)

5. Confidential Moments (A M/M Baseball romance)***

6. Clean Slates (A fast burn rock star romance)

7. Tangled Love (A rock star romance love triangle romance)

8. Restless Beat (A rock star romance)

9. Love In Sienna Boxset (Books 1-4)

10. Love in Sienna Boxset (Books 5-8)

## SENTINEL PROTECTION DUOLOGY

1. Fighting Attraction (A M/M bodyguard romance)***

2. Embracing Temptation (A M/M age gap bodyguard romance)***

## STANDALONES

Monster In The Shadows (Dark romance standalone)

Kissing in the snow (A M/M Christmas Novella set in the Sentinel Protection World)***

Afterglow (A kinky brother's best friend romance)

# ACKNOWLEDGMENTS

Thank you so much for reading Teasing the Winger.I truly hope you loved reading it!

Now onto the thank you's. There are always so many people to thank and I really hope I don't miss anyone. (But if I do I'm sorry.)

First and foremost, I want to thank my amazing team. I wouldn't be able to do any of this without them. They pick me up when I'm down and always have my back. Even though we have a business arrangement I consider them more friends than anything else. They are the hardest working women I have ever met and I am never going to let them go. So give it up for the women I couldn't live without, Brittany Franks and Suzanne Talkington!

Secondly, I want to thank my superb Alpha/Beta Readers Mandy, Robin, Shannon and Mentoah. These ladies are always pointing out the beginning issues and are always available for me to bounce ideas off of. I'd probably still be stuck trying to figure things out if it wasn't for them.

Next, my sensitivity readers for making sure that Rio and Sasha were portrayed properly. J.P Jaxson is an amazing human being that I am so lucky to call a friend and makes sure that I never miss represent the gay community. I love that he calls me out when needed and holds me to a high standard, I wouldn't want anything less. He made sure that the m/m aspects of this book were on point and he did a fantastic job. Jennifer Demeter helped with the demisexual aspect of the book and even though this was my first time working with her, I hope it isn't my last because she was fantastic to work with!

Next I want to thank my AMAZING new editor BreathlessLit. They were GREAT to work with and helped me polish this book and make it as strong as it is today.

Brittany Franks deserves her own place in the thank you's because she is really is a jack of all trades. This time around she helped proofread and really knocked it out of the park catching those pesky errors that wanted to hang on. Of course she also designed the cover for this book and as always I was blown away. Brittany is a one of a kind person and I am beyond lucky to have found her and claim her as one of my friends. She is simply the best person in the entire world. Not only is she immensely talented but she's also genuinely the most caring person I have ever met. I truly love this woman with all my heart and am NEVER letting her go.

My family for putting up with me when I put myself on a deadline and go a little crazy.

And last but obviously not least... you... the reader... without you I wouldn't be continuing to put books out! Thank you for your continued support. I love you all so much!

# ABOUT THE AUTHOR

Laura John is a steamy romance author from Alberta, Canada, who melds love and angst together while normalizing mental illness. She also brings a mixture of m/m and m/f books because love is love. In her books, you will fall in love with so many different book boyfriends it's not even funny! She really has something for everyone!

When she's not writing, she enjoys reading, going to concerts, hiking, and experimenting with makeup!

Follow Laura on social media to stay in the loop!

www.ingramcontent.com/pod-product-compliance
Lightning Source LLC
Chambersburg PA
CBHW022150240626
47153CB00007B/2602